The Perfect Circle

Pascale Quiviger
The Perfect Circle

A Novel Translated by Sheila Fischman

Cormorant Books

Canada Council **Conseil des Arts**
for the Arts **du Canada**

ONTARIO ARTS COUNCIL
CONSEIL DES ARTS DE L'ONTARIO

The publisher gratefully acknowledges the support of the Canada Council for the Arts
and the Ontario Arts Council for its publishing program. We acknowledge
the financial support of the Government of Canada through the Book Publishing
Industry Development Program (BPIDP) for our publishing activities.
Additional financial support for this translation is provided by the Canada Council
for the Arts and the Department of Canadian Heritage through the
Book Publishing Industry Development Program.

Printed and bound in Canada

LIBRARY AND ARCHIVES CANADA CATALOGUING IN PUBLICATION

Quiviger, Pascale, 1969–
[Cercle parfait. English]
The perfect circle / Pascale Quiviger; translated by Sheila Fischman. — 2nd ed.

Translation of: Le cercle parfait.
ISBN 1-897151-04-7   ISBN-13 978-1-897151-04-4

1. Fischman, Sheila 11. Title.

PS8583.U584C4713 2006A   C843'.6   C2006-905725-7

Cover design: Angel Guerra / Archetype
Text design: Tannice Goddard / Soul Oasis Networking
Cover image: Dave Nagel / Getty Images
Author Photo: Nick Pontarolo
Printer: Friesens

CORMORANT BOOKS INC.
215 SPADINA AVENUE, STUDIO 230, TORONTO, ON CANADA M5T 2C7
www.cormorantbooks.com

For those who can speak to dogs

*I*f you watch my hand move through space, you will realize that it's trying to find you.

Already it's been searching for a long time, even longer perhaps.

Touching you, it would say: I'm looking for you.

It would say: I haven't stopped loving you.

And it would say: I had to break out of your perfect circle.

THE EXACT MOMENT OF THIRST

*I*n the final scene of an Italian film, a family that's about to emigrate across the sea stops to eat on a beach. It's an ordinary day, with sun and wind. While the adults are chatting, a child climbs up the dune. Turning around when her efforts are over, she suddenly sees before her, as if for the very first time, the green sea, the blue sky, the horizon: life. She spreads her arms as wide as she can. She goes on looking for another moment.

Then tumbles down the slope, laughing, running, flying.

Your suitcase is exceptionally heavy.

"Your suitcase is too heavy," says the airline official.

Your suitcase resembles your life during these past months.

You arrive on a sweltering day. A green liqueur against a dazzling white cloth. Tall chestnut trees, their pink and fragile blossoms about to fall. You're introduced to some people having an aperitif at the bar of the small hotel. He is there, one of them, with his long beard and his amazing eyes, which you don't notice. He's drinking an *amaro* from a narrow glass that he holds cautiously in his square hands. This meeting lasts five minutes. He gets on your nerves because he talks too loud, because he has too much beard, and because of the way that he's slumped in his chair.

The first evening: chestnut honey, its flavour so dark that right away you succumb to your usual anxiety, accentuated by the fear of succumbing to your usual anxiety. Once you are inside your room, you look out the window and see a cat sprawling in the moonlight. You brush your teeth, you sit on your bed, and write: *I came here to transform fear into joy. The greatest fear into an even greater joy.*

The first night: you dream about a blue house that's collapsing. The staircases, the windows give way, and you take shelter in a yellow kitchen where a smiling man crushes sugar and shows you a window through which to escape.

The first morning: not far from the hotel there's a stone wall; behind the wall, a house; on the wall, white flowers in clumps. A woman is singing. Her song rises softly between the flowers and the sound of dishes. Now and then she walks into the house, the song is extinguished, then comes back again. She's still singing when she goes outside and shuts the garden gate.

The same day: he has cut his beard. His face is luminous, like a secret unexpectedly revealed. You're fascinated in spite of yourself by the fact that it's possible to hide such a beautiful face, as if hiding a scar. Its nakedness — more naked still because it had been hidden — testifies to a fragility similar to the fragility of birth. It is a reminder that every face is naked. It is the magnificent face of humankind. For two weeks you're careful to avoid it so that you won't be further struck by this fascination.

Two weeks later: you hear him talking with someone, telling about his father's death the year before. "It's tough, death," he says, lowering his green eyes. You don't speak to him, your hands are burning, you don't touch him. He's the kind who expresses himself by subjecting his elastic body to the maximum fatigue, by pruning language to protect what's essential. Later, in your room, you write: *Today, the outline of things close at hand was clear. Things close at hand were close at hand.*

Two days later: you go to a windy village nearby. A basilica. On the left, a door opens into the crypt. Low, dark, cool. A hexagonal crypt, a series of arches blocked by opaque white windows. Several chairs. You choose one. The wind makes a windowpane clatter, you can't tell which one, it clatters again and again, you listen to it clatter, you do nothing else. Then a strange and invisible phenomenon occurs that you won't mention to anyone.

A presence is making its way in the dark without assuming a shape. It moves along, tangible, inseparable from the wind that spreads apart the walls of the crypt. The crypt persists, turned over on itself like a big soup bowl. In the gloom the arches follow, one after another. Through one, you can sense the next. The wind is powerful. It pushes its sound along the bones that surround the womb. You wait, you close your eyes, open them, you no longer know what to focus on. The presence circles in and grabs you by the throat, at once imposing and absenting itself. This goes on for a long time, maybe an hour, maybe ten minutes. A man comes in. Points to a staircase. You climb the narrow steps, convinced that you have been there before, a thousand years ago. The banister is low, it's cut into the cold stone of the wall. The ceiling is vaulted. A small bell hangs there, covered with spider webs. At the top, a door. It opens into the church: baroque, oppressive. A little daylight comes in through the cupola. You have trouble breathing, and for several seconds you prepare yourself for the worst — for suffocation, for a flash of inspiration. You walk slowly, supernaturally, past a series of mediocre paintings and graceless statues. The circle closes near the door. A baptismal font, with water in it: you make the absurd but necessary gesture of dipping your thumb and tracing a cross on your forehead. Visitors enter and greet everyone, it's the custom. Ashamed of your damp forehead, you rush out.

Outside, the air is hot. It's the end of a sunny afternoon. People are walking along the street. You realize that inside it was cold, that you felt cold. You understand everything then, you understand because of the dark memory of a more ancient cold. The womb, the wind that smashes, that waits. The man who shows you the exit, the narrow tunnel at the end of which you breathe awkwardly. Daylight through the cupola, and the baptismal cross.

You walk. You stop at a wall that's as compact as a slab of stone. Yellow moss covers it. You place your hand on it. You think: my father was a wall. So be it. It was his way of being a father, unshakeable. Of protecting the womb from the wind that smashes. Of protecting the child who emerged from the dark. First meeting. First love. In the womb, love hadn't appeared yet, because the child and the womb were identical. You think about the arms that guard the child's first sleep. After the Fall those arms are absolute, the first place of understanding that is separate from oneself. Though silent themselves, they invite confidence, they promise to resist the wind, the weather, the womb. I will be there, always, I will be like a wall, like your wall, I will be your wall, now sleep. I will be the one who doesn't fall.

The same day: you realize that the walls are made of stone. The same day, you close your eyes and can't think of the word for that which emerges. You have an urge to pray and to cry, you realize that you know nothing about yourself. You're outside, in broad daylight, in a public place, a foreign country, and you look like a madwoman.

It is in spite of yourself that you fall in love. You have to know that through the open window the blossoming chestnut tree enters your room and that water here always tastes of lemon. Above all, it's necessary to know that between their spread petals can be seen something never seen before: the palpable desire of flowers. And that finally you sense inside yourself something you'd never felt before: the power to be a bouquet.

You fall in love with despair, when there's not much time left in this journey that's nearly over, and with the agonizing thought of the life that awaits you on the other continent, known in advance, carefully planned, and the thought of the companion with whom for years you've been sharing your bed, doing the dishes, and speaking a common language, a language slowly constructed and remarkably tender.

He comes for you in the middle of the night and guides you towards extremely violent hot springs. The car's headlights cling to the haze of bodies. Dozens of ghostly shadows pierce the mist. The water is as hot as fever. One man's hand tries to find the buttocks of every woman while he, farther along, walks confidently on the slippery stones. The landscape seems to open up as an extension of his movement. In the middle of the night, in the middle of the cascades: he sits down beside you. You've been expecting what is happening now, and you doubt it in the same way you'd doubt a mirage. Which is to say: not in the least. Which is to say: absolutely.

A single movement is all it takes for your whole life to fall apart — the movement of clinging to his ankle instead of to the face of the rock. Your whole being held in check by this man's ankle under water that's galloping and howling, your life exported towards a dark and wonderful point — far from any available lexicon.

The next day: to your great surprise, you step spontaneously outside the circle before it closes in. You escape by train, as far north as possible. Not knowing that your fascination with this country will be added to that of his face and will merge with it; not knowing that you are enlarging the circle, making it more able to keep you inside it.

Italy is the fact of finding a fountain at the exact moment of thirst.

Women are slim in their tight little dresses, men look at them and the day starts early. The mallet of the sun climbs up the walls and brings out the rough parts in minute detail. Brightness prowls from east to west, it persists from January through December, and one marvels that the months in the year still number twelve. Open doors and closed shutters, restaurants that overflow onto the street. The all-consuming heat of afternoon, the salty leftovers from *pranzo*, and the wind, always the wind, sometimes barely thin, sometimes paunchy, sometimes raging; in one minute transformed into a storm, into hail that falls onto the summer. At dawn, the happy aroma of coffee, at noon, the warm smell of frying, and at sunset, the round perfume of all the flowers together, motionless and invisible under the dust of the sky.

Skins are dark, hands quick to settle on the other, to squeeze an arm, to not listen. Everyone talks at once. While others laugh and concoct little lies, memory accumulates on top of objects, in thick sediments that will become sunflowers, that will become, soon, the dull ochre colour of the bare walls. They know how long history is. They know that they are merely the still-alive stratum of all those memories accumulated by a people. They talk about nothing, but they talk outside. Speech is inflated on public squares, the women go outside in slippers to sweep the street. Memory swells, rises up to a sky that's incendiary at three in the afternoon, healing at midnight.

Italy is the secret voices of vespers in a church that's patched together like a soul. It is the pink, pale sun of a slow Sunday on a *piazza del Duomo*, the sermon that leaks outside and sits at the Communist terrace of the café next door. It is the oldest covered theatre in the world, with a *trompe l'oeil* painting of three streets in Thebes. It is the blue humanism of Giotto that beats like a heart, the immortal gazes of men and women on human mortality, the aching eye of Judas as he is betraying Christ, the plunge of Jonah whose robe becomes a fish; it is the circle of water around John the Baptist, and Mary knowing in advance that she will lose everything.

It is the wild capers growing on the outer wall, picked by children from the tops of ladders. It is the *oculus* in the

Pantheon, two thousand years of stars, moons, and rain. It is March 28, 1171, in Ferrara, the blood that spurts from the Host, spatters the priest, stains the ceiling, and guarantees the parish a fixed revenue from pilgrims yet to come, world without end. It is, in that same church, the true miracle of the sun making a chair stand out while an old nun sweeps the floor against a background of Beethoven.

And it is the casual way of centuries that are super-imposed, the certainty that this country, which has existed from time immemorial, will not disappear. Outward-bound frescoes, three one-armed, decapitated saints, naïve faces streaked with grey plaster, garments half torn-off a missing body. Blood-red lines obstinately running onto the fabric of robes, tracing prematurely or belatedly the geography of a colour yet to come, a colour that's leaving. And above the Holy Family in exile, the imprint of the sun has just lain down, its arms outstretched; it accompanies, murmuring, the wreckage of the stone, the retrenchment of images into a memory more and more remote. It is the contemporary sun, extremely and mathematically precise, that snaps us up in the concrete history of the precise texture of things.

Italy is scattered with places of prayer and revenge, of art and power. Its open churches soliloquize in the ear of the first person who comes along. You don't know anyone, you listen to churches. You observe the sky manufactured by hands and you hear the human heart breathing within the origin of its prayer.

Timidly you touch the characters that are ahead of themselves and they strike you as fragile under the gruelling helmet of humid life, fragile just as we all are. You make your way into the ports of call towards the sure and splendid end of white-shirted encounters around a welcoming table. Crossing Venice without consulting a map, you emerge into the sudden coolness of a small street, and above your shoulders the sky is hardly wider than a fishing line. Your eyes are constantly learning how to see. You walk Italy, won over by age-old patience and already happy because of a word, tossed off among others, red and salty like the first meal, *buon giorno* — welcome to the country of everyone.

Without your knowing it, as you expand the circle of fascination you reduce by the same amount your chances of escaping it.

Going back to your room you note that the chestnut blossoms have fallen off the tree and that in their fall, they've crushed the delicate architecture of petals, pistils, sugar. What is left on the branches: balls covered with sharp points and at their tips, drying like a navel, is the old stem of the flower under which they were sleeping. The chestnuts now resemble land-mines.

You no longer eat, no longer speak. You're stunned that you've been transformed so quickly into moss, into stone, into explosive. You catch a glimpse of the extreme violence of the happiness to come and of its end, which is folded inside its beginning.

The night after your return: he sits with you in the garden of the hotel. The night is warm in the deserted garden. He asks you if you'd rather be alone, he asks you if you believe in God. Without waiting for the answer, he loads his dogs into the Jeep and takes you to another village for a drink. The full moon over a bridge. The wish you make is to hold back time. A storm bursts, and together you run into the night of the yellow streets. On the way back, while mud erupts onto the windows, he looks at you with a strange smile. Then thanks you, you'll never know for what, maybe for taking the plane all the way to him and for slipping into this unlikely encounter.

It's a story like so many others, a cheap little story, perhaps, but a living soul would gladly shatter itself in one that's even cheaper.

You don't see him the next day or the next. He is protecting himself from your imminent departure. Waiting for him to show up at any street corner, you think you'll go mad. He knows places where you'll never find him. He knows all the ones where he can find you. At last, he comes. You spend a night in the garden. You spend a second night on the floor of an empty house filled with the fragrance of rosemary. He unrolls a mattress to place beneath desire. All night and until the flowered floor tiles emerge from the dimness, his tired hand walks on you, pulls the prickly blanket over your shoulder when you're asleep, when you aren't asleep. Always, he holds you in his hands as if to keep you from flying away. His hair is soaked in sweat; he says, laughing, that it's because rain fell through the roof. He doesn't sleep. Dawn breaks on his open eyes and he gets up with the dawn. His nakedness is like a child's: the most natural, most comfortable, least shameful state. His body is thickset, dark, sturdy, gathered into padded muscles, and the barely wakened sky traces its pink shape through the open window. You leave for France. He thinks you'll never come back and therefore he asks you for nothing. He picks up his watch from the floor and with that abrupt way he has of disappearing, that will cause you so much suffering later on, he tells you that you can go back to sleep or go back to the hotel, as you think best. He gets dressed, covers you, and goes out, leaving the door open.

Contrary to all expectations, his or yours, you will come back. You'll come back because in the empty house he didn't sleep. Because you will be anguished by his anguish and by his nakedness projected into the dawn, pink and indecent.

You leave for France. Your face is undone. A cousin says so right away, before you've opened your mouth, "You're in love, it shows, you don't know what to do." You're invited to the tables of all Brittany and can't even swallow your spit.

He turned you to jelly with such ease. He did very little to seduce you. But that very little, in front of the bouquet prepared in secret and so long before, was worth more than a promise. You see his face on every clump of earth and in every field of artichokes and on the seafront too, at Pointe du Raz. Your thoughts give way before that appalling image, now you can't gather it into one clear and lucid moment, a moment during which a road might open. You shower three times a day. At night, you listen to music with your eyes wide open. You spend months of salary on the phone with the companion from that other life awaiting you in Quebec. You tell him everything. He answers with words that you thought were reserved for literature. "Go, I love you. It hurts me to say this, but I wish you a bon voyage."

You're alone, terribly alone, in this freedom both of them are offering you — the one by letting you go, the other by not waiting for you. Perhaps you'd never been alone before, from now on, no doubt, you always will be. You're alone, without good or evil, without fear or shame. You are alone to the degree that you're terribly free, with a new and shattering freedom, and you don't know how to formulate your law; you're perplexed as would be a slave who's set free overnight. You put off and put off making your decision. At the very last minute, you set off for Italy again. Three weeks.

The cousin pays for your train ticket. A train that charges into the night, into your night, burrowing into it. You don't know what this night will consist of. But you want to know the truth, you want your heart to be as clean and clear as the sun in the water.

That week, floods in northern Italy. The train has to change its route, and at dawn a man opens hysterically the door to your compartment and wakes you up, gesticulating to make you get out, repeating in the language that you don't yet know, *alluvione*, his fingers pointing to a map, and because of that, for a long time you think *alluvione* means river. You run along the platform, repeating the name of a station to all the ticket inspectors and finally you end up, breathless and ticketless, on another train, and then on the station platform where he's supposed to be waiting for you.

You call him at home three times, but he's not there. It's a day of strong winds and he's on the lake with his sailboard, while you wait for him on the deserted platform, half understanding — though you won't admit it to yourself — that you'll always be waiting for him. Half understanding that suffering while you wait for him will hardly matter compared with your passionate love. You smoke four or five cigarettes in quick succession, stubbing them in the grass beside a fountain. The day is hot, windy. A man with a scarred face approaches, you send him packing. He arrives late, unsmiling, hair wet from the lake. Some distance down the road, he finally murmurs, not looking at you: "I'm glad you came back." Poppies appear under the big sky.

That night and all the nights after it: you sleep in his arms. At five o'clock every morning he gets dressed without waking you up and sneaks out of the hotel. The days are long and torrid, you walk in the village alone, and at the hour when people come home from work, you bathe in the blue bathroom, all the windows open, using soap that smells of apricots — of which you keep a piece in anticipation of your old age, when you'll need a souvenir that hasn't grown old.

Every evening: you wait for him outside while, as the daylight is waning, the wind works at breaking the teeth of the flowers and the world is like a big basket of oranges from which you pick a chair. You listen to the voices, varied, bushy, speaking the foreign language, and now and then a word that you recognize leaps like a fish. You know that he'll come but you don't know when. The evenings are numbered. One day, you asked him what he'd seen in you. He told you: "So many things." You said: "Name me just one." He named serenity. The answer surprised you; you told him so. "It's a matter of time," he replied. While you wait for him that serenity is there with you, sitting beside you. It's sad and strange, and he was the first to see it.

He arrives late, takes you out for supper, makes you laugh. After supper, he follows you to your room. Because you're an unexpected visitor at the peak of the tourist season, you've had to switch rooms several times. Your beds are no one's beds, they are borrowed, creaking, uncomfortable. You put the mattress on the floor so you won't make any noise. Lying against you, he speaks more slowly. The room, the window, his face, the mattress flow together in the dim light. All you can see is the lunar brightness of his teeth that bite you, smiling, while sweat runs back up the course of his skin. Your hands are his hands are your hands. Everything is done in silence on the floors of these rooms. He works at breaking your life by making it possible — one day you will be there where *here* should be.

The days: you spend them alone, a silhouette that moves expectantly through the sounds of cars and the furtive voice of the lake. At the washhouse, the women chat while they slap their husbands clothes against the stone. Deep in the clear rinse water, soap deposits stand out against pieces of shadow that tremble in the sun. In the water, the garments stretch, as if emerging slowly from a deep sleep. Behind the castle, the women hang their washing on a very long line, so long that it has to be supported in the middle with a branch shaped like a slingshot. The installation looks terribly precarious and yet, when the garments offer their soft cheeks to the approaching wind, the slingshot sways with perfect ease, like a pendulum that operates counter to the pull of gravity. You offer your own cheek and remember certain warm events, such as the old man who says, though he doesn't know you: "You must live every day as if it were the last and then you must sleep well every night."

In your bag you have an Italian grammar which you work hard at deciphering. On the shore of the lake every morning, you choose the ugliest spot because it's in the shade and no one else is there. Leaning against a cement wall, you open your grammar, recognize in it some words from the night before and you learn other words that you'll recognize in people's mouths that very evening. The language allows itself to be penetrated, puts up not much more resistance than butter, as if it were submitting to the urgency of being learned.

When you go out with him he talks with others, while under the table his hand is on your knee. One night he invites you to a party at the castle. Along a narrow street, a table has been set up, with Chinese lanterns of every colour swaying above it. The wine arrives in pitchers, the pasta, the salad, the meat in huge pots. People quarrel, embrace, lean out windows; children race around under the tables, on top of the tables, everywhere. Guided by his hand on your knee, that evening you realize that you understand Italian.

You do nothing but that — walk, study the language, draw, wait for him, hate him because of the waiting, yet smile at him as soon as he arrives. Because you say nothing, do nothing, except at night, except make love, your senses are abruptly sharpened. Listening to the water, you can erase the boundaries of your skin and move into the great body of the lake. You see with appalling precision the skeleton of a tree that stands out against the six o'clock sky. From a handful of sand you feel each grain leak between your splayed fingers. You notice the cold aroma of fortified wine and, pretty well everywhere, the smell of the detergent his mother uses. You scrutinize the ever-changing light, you see it more and more clearly, in every possible state, even at night when it crawls. Behind your senses that are sharpened to the extreme, stands for the first time the present tense, and it has two arms, like a whale.

During the years that separated you from childhood, you lived in expectation of the present tense, but it never came. And yet while age walks over it, childhood remains, faithful, close at hand, ready to speak its feverish language as long as you pay attention to it. Because you knew that childhood was very close, you expected time would once again be what it had been then: the present, eternity. You applied yourself to waiting, paying attention to a host of details, but you had only a relative success, similar to the kind obtained from studying books. Because of it, now, which lays down mountains instead of craters, and lakes in the most arid parts of the globe, because of it, abruptly, that childhood talent comes back to you, intact. You know that you'll go away again. Soon. There are five days left, on the next day, four. There is the paradoxical coincidence of the passing days and the new-found present tense. You are there, in the middle, in the form of a still, distilling time so as to capture its essence.

He talks to you a lot about his mother, whom he lives with. He never takes you there.

The tension of this happiness to be lost has you in a continuous *crescendo*. Secretly you hope he'll ask you never to leave. But because he is made in such a way that he never says more than is necessary, he'll never say enough. He considers that life goes on above thoughts, and that while it's going on it becomes what a life should be. For the last days, you are moved to a vast, deserted dormitory in a wing of the hotel that's set aside for one-week stays by mental patients. It's dark there, footsteps reverberate, and voices move from one floor to the next, distorted by the echo. Crazy among the crazies, you sense your thought process skidding beneath itself, every second forming incongruous plans such as staying for another month, such as leaving as soon as you can, such as dying or making a baby. Wakings are breathtakingly painful. They take you by surprise in that hollow which, when sleeping, forgets to defend itself, forgets to close its fist. It's the hollow he conquered, an infinitely fragile place. It is there that he lets you decide about everything. You watch your own madness develop, watch it feed largely on itself and hardly at all on him. He always does the same little bit, but you take that little bit and transform it effortlessly into a poem, a Greek tragedy, a cosmological myth. You see that and you go on, because your own madness fascinates you — as much as his body, as much as his country.

He's asleep, of course, on the last night when you finally make up your mind. You pack your bags while listening to the footsteps of a madman walking down the corridor. The plane leaves from Paris. The suitcase is still just as heavy. You'll have to take a train from Florence, get to Florence from the closest railroad station, travel to that station on the bus that leaves the village every morning before sunrise. At four a.m. you wake him up. He sees the suitcase. He speaks to you in Italian, then repeats it in French.

"Don't forget," he says.

You promise. It's a superfluous promise. Everything is engraved as if in wood, in copper, in marble: chestnut blossoms, the wind in the crypt, the languor of the garments in the washhouse basin. His own face, which the light revealed all at once in its sudden nakedness, and the promised serenity: yours, your own possible serenity.

You board the bus, the first train, the second train. Between Florence and Paris the night is dreadful. Hot. The vinyl couchette sticks to your legs whenever the sheet slides off. Sheets always slide off vinyl. In your half-sleep the nightmare sound of other passengers who converse and guffaw in the overheated alcohol vapours. A Roman priest speaks slowly, thinks slowly, an Englishman listens to himself say nothing between his flabby mouth and his harelip, three Americans jump from one subject to another, always on the surface of things, while you do battle with the devil, and the kilometres shriek along the rails. You get up and step outside the compartment. You wish you were eighty-three so you could avoid the inevitable and prepare yourself, calmly, in your rocking chair, to sleep for a very long time. There's no space for crying. Near the toilets, the doors open behind your back; in the corridor, someone jostles you. You rest your head on the glass through which the legendary countryside streams by with a metallic crashing, until the train enters France, your father's country, which he left thirty years earlier, for love. You are leaving now to conclude what your life used to be. You don't know anything else. You can't say whether by taking the train again, you've lost love or preserved it. As she leaves the toilet, a Dutch woman's gaze locks with your red eyes and she gives you a knowing sorry smile, the only presence of that entire night.

In Paris, you board the plane. In Montreal, you take in your arms the other, who is crying, and together you undress your house, cut it into two scrupulously equal parts which each of you moves by yourself, elsewhere. You keep the Scrabble set and the Moroccan cookbook, the other takes the Bescherelle and Madame Benoît.

The first weeks, you spend inside, among the unopened boxes, waiting for the moment when you'll have the courage to select a book and lose yourself in it. It goes on all summer. At summer's end you realize that you haven't had enough money for a long time now. You take any old job — sales, telephone survey, whatever. You write to him every week, he never replies. For yourself, you also write: *The distance between beings who are thinking about one another, who don't know where the other is or what he's doing, who trust and who lose confidence, is something extraordinary. I absolutely have to stop smoking.*

And so September passes; in October, you stop smoking. Everything strikes you as totally dull, without interest. At the beginning of November, you stop being faithful to him. At the end of November, he calls you. On the phone, in a second at most, his country enters your kitchen and excavates once more the lost dimension. You become yesterday again, in the basket of oranges, on a muddy road where a storm has broken. His voice carries flowers in these early days of winter. He asks you to come back, you say no, you hang up hastily. Twenty-four hours later you borrow the money your brother's been saving to pay his taxes and you buy a plane ticket. You start counting the days again.

You spend December in a three-storey apartment that he rents for you in the centre of the village and where he leaves you alone all day and sometimes even all night. It's cold, damp, grey. You hardly ever see him and you don't understand his absence. Neither of you can find a way to put together the pieces of the previous summer, swallowed up by the silence of autumn, dissolved in anger and infidelity. Yet your fascination with him sinks in like a nail, you are at once happy and broken, unable to make sense of yourself, you go round and round in circles inside the three storeys of the cold house, in the rainy village, every day feeling chillier in both body and soul, every day more confused. You think he's magnificent. From saying them over and over to yourself, you wear out in your head the few words he's set down for you between the dark sheets, you strip them off like petals, one by one, you measure them to determine whether or not they'll compensate for his absence. They never do.

One night, anger wakes you with a start. You dress in the dark and go to the harbour where violent winds threaten to uproot the seaweed. You howl. Carried away by the powerful sound of the water, your voice founders, inaudible. You go to his place. You don't know the address but you recognize the dark roses he's told you about, and his dogs greet you with a tumultuous joy that is absolutely unwarranted. A light comes on. He steps outside in slippers and briefs. With the harshest words you know in his language, which you learned from him as it happens, you turn him into a pillar of salt and dump him there, standing between his mother's rosebushes, in the icy murmur of the lake. You're crazy about this man. With the kind of craziness that absence has sharpened to a razor's edge, you'd like to make him bleed to death. He doesn't reply, there's the usual delay between thinking something and expressing it, while you turn around and stomp back to your damp house. He's been demolished. He'll tell you so, much later.

It snows in the village for the first time in forty years, on that very night. The snow sticks to the rough stones of the medieval walls like mushrooms on the trunks of trees. It comes up to the eyes of windows, opened now and then by someone who sticks out a hand to check that it's really true. You have the frivolous impression that the snow is falling just for you so you can start writing your story again on a blank page. You have the impression that the sky is trying to make your two countries resemble one another. The snow brings out a smile as familiar as a school bell. He comes for you around noon, stammering. You agree to follow him to the house of a friend where the pipes are frozen.

Familiarity with snow restores human activities to their proper proportions. The villagers don't possess that habit. The women stay inside, arms folded, brows knit, fearing unknown dangers for their men. The men go outside bareheaded, blasphemy streams from between their frozen ears. They insist on driving their cars, skid on the road, get lost in snowdrifts. Laughing nervously, they step on the gas, then give up, slamming the car door, and walk back home where just this once, the mothers themselves get out the bottle of grappa. Only children and dogs seem to understand what snow is really made of. Snow is made of water transformed into a school holiday, a village-wide amusement park, it's a bee that melts on their tongues, it's the sudden presence of both parents at the same time. The children run with the dogs, crying out, they roll on the ground, and get their boots full of it.

People count on the sun to get rid of the snow. Heating systems and pipes are frozen, the power lines give up. You go with him through the village on a lengthy round of emergency repairs. He spends the day explaining that you have to keep a trickle of water running, and lecturing to clients who've refused to invest in a better system. By giving him a chance to help out others, the storm also allows him to make a promotional tour. He doesn't let anyone pay because he knows when he goes to Giuseppe's that he is guaranteeing himself easy acquisition of the next hunting permit, and that by going to Massimo's, he'll get free seeds for his mother's garden. You observe all that and you understand that he moves in a limited space where every person is connected to all the others by a kind of economic intermarriage, by the reassuring burden of mutual survival, by an archaic debt that lies dormant behind every window in the village, behind every face.

In the yard behind the hotel, where you finally go for a coffee, a path has been dug out with a spoon that's just wide enough for one pair of legs; its edges crumble as you walk on it. After your coffee you go to the harbour. It's already night and snow is still falling. The sky is a peculiar blue, as if the white earth were going to force it to speak. Masts sing in the wind, the sound more crystalline than usual. He lets his white dogs run in the white harbour, between snowballs.

The storm lasts for two days. Because of it perhaps, you become inseparable — or because your anger has been purged. It's also because of the giddiness you take from one another that neither silence nor distance nor anger can appease. He lends you a coat and boots, stays close to you and, with no apology or explanation, he draws you gently back into the circle of love; you go along with it because it's good that way, because the force that propels you towards him comes from very high, because you'll give anything to allow that force to act.

When the snow has melted you go back to Quebec. You write to him every week, every day, every hour, every minute, over a period of seven months. You write about this and that, but in fact you only write about one thing, the distance between you and the slow passage of time. *I want to tell you things I don't know how to say in your language and that you can't read in mine, things that while I wait should perhaps be kept silent so they'll watch over us in secret, so that on this side of us, they will take care of the road our souls follow towards each other, blindly, so that one day, finally, our continents will be absolved.*

He calls you once a month, Saturday morning on the stroke of eight. The conversation lasts for seven or eight minutes, scarcely long enough to recognize your voice and adjust to the language used, long enough to understand that he really does exist, that he always will exist, and that because of you, he can't sleep. Obsessed by his calls, you develop a scientific interest in how telephones work — and satellites and cables in general. Obsessed by him, you don't do the slightest thing without dedicating it secretly to him, you don't say a single word without wishing that he could hear it.

A person can write this, it's easy enough: "You are waiting for him." But the wait is long enough to invent the wheel, to pass through the Middle Ages, produce the Renaissance, count on Modernity, and then give up on everything, end the millennium as if one were closing a bad book, opening it again only to throw it in the fire. When one day he invites you to come back, you accept.

You don't want to live through another departure that contains a return. You leave your job and your apartment, wipe out your bank account, give away a few things and store the rest, tell your friends goodbye. All this you do with bitter lucidity, with a premonition that you're flying towards failure, but knowing too, knowing powerfully, that this probable failure is coupled with some dark truth. To bring that truth within your grasp, you empty out your known world and fill up your suitcase again. It is for that truth, far more than for him, that you decide to leave and to balance yourself on the instinctive crest, with nothing behind you and nothing ahead, and without a net to guard against falls.

You board the plane on June 1. Twenty-seven years after your birth, fifty-two years after Hiroshima, four hundred and ninety-five years after Michelangelo sculpted his *David*, four months before your godson's birth. You board the plane, it would be an event of no significance if such events existed. Such events do not exist.

For some time I thought that this story would be my entire life. Maybe I wasn't mistaken. This story, brief though it may be, led me towards the precise point at which living should result from a decision. You would make everything possible by making everything impossible, everything but the exhausting memory of intense joy.

I would like to make of this story an object, I would like that object to be a book. I would change all the names, all but the dogs'. That way I could set it down somewhere, in my bedroom maybe but outside myself, and I could close my eyes and sleep.

And I could sleep.

Those words last only long enough to lose you.

I

THE POSSIBLE PLACE

*B*eauty makes us solitary. It makes us responsible for tolerating its passing and for being its worthy witnesses.

I am looking for nothing else.

The problem is that of disappearance. Beauty always goes away. As a child, I wanted to be equal to that departure and I felt very deeply that to achieve it, I would have to do something with beauty, perhaps something that doesn't die. But all things perish and it's when we learn this that we take leave of our childhood.

The problem remains intact. The heavy joy of beauty will be nowhere except in itself and it will leave me alone, here, leave me only myself shot through with beauty, unless I do something with it.

Unless I do something with beauty.

Marco is thirty-seven when Marianne meets him, he's drinking an *amaro* from a narrow glass, he's wearing a white T-shirt, he has a long beard.

He lives in a village on a hill, beside a lake. The stone is ochre and grey, the place emerges from its walls and seems to want to hoist itself above them. From the highest point, behind the castle's battlements, emerge the triangular façade of the church with its steeple on the right and on the left the ghost of another, which fell during the war. The scales of unambitious children practising on the municipal piano hover above the central square, which you reach through narrow labyrinths where doors and windows open in the most incongruous places. Silk underwear is quite conspicuously hung out to dry, plants climb up staircases, icons sit in niches carved into the walls, plastic Virgins, artificial flowers, portraits of saints dog-eared from the rain. Dishevelled straw-bottomed chairs sit here and there, sown at random. From all the openings, in what appears to be a single immense house, can be heard laughter and shouting, radios, dubbed American soaps, and the figures who are stubbornly impassive before a stranger become animated and excited in the company of neighbours. The village is round, closed, but three lookouts open onto the lake and the uninformed stroller plunges into a windy vertigo there, as if vigorously regaining the use of a lung.

Higher up, in the wild grass of the hill, Roman ruins disclose an underground passage, site of orgiastic worship; a well filled with ferns; an altar; and the clear outline of what was once a temple, with steps, monumental, that point to the highest part of the sky. Close by in the cemetery, tombstones stubbornly display the same three family names, and the gate creaks like the caretaker's knees when he comes to open it, chewing candies.

An alley of plane trees goes down from villa to villa, all the way to the lake at the bottom of which, according to legend, lies an Etruscan village. Professional fishermen leave at night wearing woollen caps and come back around nine or ten in the morning. Their boats are inspired by the Etruscan model, with a wide, flat bottom that keeps them from capsizing. They have a tapered bow and a wide stern and Marco thinks they're "as beautiful as a woman's thighs." The lake, which is volcanic, is clear and blue and tepid. In September, the water is turned over by the *tramontana* and its icy bottom comes up to the surface. Among the villagers it invokes fearful respect and a jealous affection. On average, two tourists drown in it every year.

The patron saint of the village is a little guy whose martyrdom is recreated every year on the public square. He is torn apart in front of the main bar; when the blood flows onto his white robe, the crowd shudders, then applauds when he refuses to recant. When he finally succumbs, angels — muscular, tanned, bare-chested, bare-legged — come to fetch him under a shower of petals.

Marianne meets Marco at the hotel bar one night. The next day she sees the light on his face for the first time.

As a child I used to lie in the grass and use the garden hose to soak the earth. I liked the smell of the swarming universe and of the life mounting up the green stems. It was the smell — I didn't know it at the time — of the house you were preparing to close up and would unlock years later as a place where we could pass the night.

There are the hours of waiting for you and then the ones spent not waiting.

There are the hours spent letting you disappear.

You made the sky immense and brought it closer for me. Every day when I wake up I will thank you for it.

When Marco asks Marianne to come and live in his country, he has the electricity reconnected in the house of his childhood which has been uninhabited since he built a more spacious one in the new part of the village. Marianne knows the old house without ever having seen it. She's been inside it already, to lie on the floor and to not sleep. She knows only odours — of the rosemary her shoulder has brushed against at the entrance to the garden, of a dark room, of sleeping Europe, of the earth that drinks the rain, of damp cellars; she knows the thrilling smell of Marco's skin, the steel smell of his sweat, the blank smell of his silence.

When Marianne decides to move in with Marco, he opens the windows and the dampness is scattered outside.

The house is squeezed into the back of a garden that's cluttered and crammed on all sides — right, left, above, behind — by other, similar houses that sit, neglected, under the mild sky; it has a flat roof, narrow windows, and walls where the plaster is eroding in patches. Long ago, all these houses belonged to Marco's grandfather, a very prosperous fisherman who made his fortune by sending out other village men to fill their boats with eels and whitefish for him. He had a nasal voice, he drank a lot, was always joking, and smoked too much. One day in his youth, during a fierce storm, he set off for one of the five islands, where he seduced a girl, brought her back to the village, and married her without further ado. When he was old and deaf and one of his grandsons came to introduce his fiancée, he started to cry because he couldn't hear her voice. He died while playing cards, holding a spectacular hand. He brought his progeny to live in row houses, but before he died he sold them one after another. Marco bought the one where he'd spent his childhood with his father, his mother, his brother, his grandparents, and an aunt. The Germans had occupied it too, during the Second World War.

Now the house is empty. No longer is it home to children's cries, dogs' stories or German barking, or to the table under which Marco's brother used to tie him up, unbeknownst to anyone. The aunt with whiskers lives in an institution and the grandfather is dead. The empty house has three windows and two doors, and the shifting shadows of those who used to live there sometimes move around on the twelve strokes of noon. Marco doesn't talk about it, but Marianne senses that she's being pushed into someone's inviolable privacy. There is no table, chair or hot water, and in the bedroom hangs a curtain his mother wanted put up, to shield their love-making from the neighbours' curiosity. As for the armoire that belonged to the grandmother, she is advised not to touch it.

A few weeks after Marianne's arrival, Marco, suddenly tired of playing fakir on the bedsprings, decides to buy a mattress. He drives the Jeep into town. He chooses a double-bed mattress that's wider than the roof of his car. He brings it to the village on the roof anyway, constantly checking it with his left hand to make sure that it won't fall off. The mattress finds its place in the middle of the bedroom, doubled in the mirror of the armoire where Marco likes to see his own reflection carrying Marianne's off to sleep. It's a mattress wider than a car, wider than the village, it some-times spills over the vineyards and the entire universe, it is a flying mattress. It becomes the heart of the house, its beating. Marco leaves it at five every morning, already tired from his too-short night.

Around, in front, behind, on both sides, and above, live aunts, uncles, and cousins of Marco's. The aunt from up above knocks on the door the first morning and under the pretext of looking for a kitten, she's come to solve the mystery of the electricity that's come back on after ten years of darkness. By noon, Marco's mother already knows that the aunt has seen Marianne, already knows what she thinks of her. It's a family of people who fish for a living. From the telephone lines that transmit the meagre information obtained by a sustained process of listening through walls and observing at windows, they weave their nets. Those nets are invisible. Marianne, who's naïve enough to think that she is free of everything, doesn't immediately realize that the place is haunted and that it will conjure up another space — her own, the biggest, the smallest, the space without furniture, where voices reverberate, banging their heads against the wall.

Because the house watches over a cold truth, impossible to embrace, which will stand before her every day, every night; which will surprise her at every waking with the burning acuity of liquid nitrogen; that truth, the only one, with its abrupt corners and the broken voice of a weary angel; that truth is the kernel of her solitude. And it is precisely by cracking that kernel, filled with hope, that Marianne will discover it's empty, empty with a windy emptiness that passes through the body and erases the soul, that takes from one's hands all the tools of joy. Then she'll start listening to music, perhaps for the first time she will really listen to music — in other words, needing it. She'll stretch out on the big mattress in the afternoon — no one's looking for her, no one's calling for her — she'll listen to requiems that will open cathedrals of glass, then she will fall half asleep, outside time, finally dissolved in the song that saves her and for a moment draws her out of her agitation. She will always be surprised when the music expires, because in the end it's only a sixty-minute cassette; surprised when reality, painful, crashes down on her again like a sledgehammer as soon as the silence resumes its rights.

And that is how she'll succumb to cigarettes again.

The narrow cul-de-sac that's pink in the morning and green at night bears the name of a great navigator. In Marianne's garden there's a plum tree, in the neighbour's on the left, a pear tree, further away two olive trees and a peach tree, further still there are vines climbing up wooden trellises, and at the very end, a stand of fig trees, weeds and roses. An underground spring runs into a canal dug by each family to dip water from it — an undertaking worthy of ancient Rome that makes it possible to grow flowers with no increase in taxes. On windy nights in July, each garden deposits in the leaves its own resonance, which is more or less subdued, more or less laden with flowers and oil, sometimes crystallized in the voices of children or interrupted by the growls of a poodle that never recognizes anyone. All the residents pick from the same fig tree, greet the same child, silence the same dog, as if they were part of a single entity, as if they shared a secret that really consists of nothing more than a key in their pockets.

One of the oldest roads in Europe crosses the village. Cars speed along it. At the edge of the pavement, dusty plastic bouquets here and there commemorate a death, forming a kind of sparse, anonymous rosary. When the villagers arrive from outside the village, even if they've only been away for a few hours, they can't stop themselves from taking the ritual detour that starts on the main road, goes down the avenue of plane trees and along the lake, then back up to the road. Along the footpath circling the lake are scattered a myriad bars. Inevitably an acquaintance has stopped at one of them, so they stop as well, or toot their horns. Often the evening outing will be nothing more than this trip around the block, all windows open, scanning the terraces.

At the edge of the lake, set back, is a beach of coloured pebbles, shards of plates and glass, polished tiles; offshore, the cabin of a half-sunk yacht serves as a diving board for children. A maritime pine — stiff, bent in two like someone with a terrible stomach ache — dips its head, kept from falling by a metal post. In a park, a seesaw, a slide, a fountain, and some benches, as well as a clock that always shows the right time, the only punctual clock in the village, giving the impression that time, motionless elsewhere, only starts up again in this very spot, under the eyes of children watched over by the old. Across the way, all summer long there's an amusement park. Its few rusty rides make a terrible racket. Now and then a teenaged couple kiss on the swaying seats of the Ferris wheel that the operator starts up just for them and which go by so quickly that no one can make them out, and they themselves can't pick out on the face of the other the joyous turmoil brought on by proximity. A pathetic place, artificial, a temporary Eden — at the far end of the grounds you can see the two magic vans it emerged from and will disappear into during the first days of September.

The avenue that runs along the lakeshore is guarded by pine trees. The sun falls like powder, resembles the light in Renaissance paintings — white in the distance, yellow up close. Trees are planted at random, with no alignment, giant parasols from which thorns rain down. Between the paved street and the carpet of thorns there's no sidewalk, no border, nothing to indicate the limit between the street and the rest and, in the end, everything is the street, nothing is the street, strollers travel on the pavement and cars, between the pines.

The harbour consists of a few circles of oil meandering between some pleasure craft and a dozen sailboats. Off to one side, a boat of no precise colour is docked in water so shallow you can see its outline on the mud. An orphan boat, and honest. On its side are peeling layers of paint that testify to its age like tree rings. Families of ducks drift by it and human families come to watch them. As for the fishermen's impeccable boats, they are moored to the wharf on the right, the order different every day depending on when they've come in. All bear the name of a woman — which is not necessarily that of the fisherman's wife. Maurizio, for instance, bought his boat from a brother of his wife's and to his great despair it bears the name of his mother-in-law. Massimo's boat and Sergio's are both called *Anna Maria* and while you might assume that this not-uncommon name belongs to two different women, everyone knows that actually, it's the same one.

Anna Maria is a cousin of Marco's mother. Thirty years earlier she was slim and brunette, she had straight teeth like all the members of her family, and her long fingers lent the same grace to washing the dishes or to playing the piano — by her own admission, she'd never played anything but the C major and D major scales, though legend had heard her play with brio some operatic arias. Massimo had fallen head-over-heels in love with her the day he'd seen her hang up red silk underwear from her window. His courtship was persistent and thoughtful, highlighted by the christening of his brand new boat, which was painted the same red as her briefs. But Anna Maria, amply wooed though she was only a fisherman's daughter, knew that she had enough cards in her hand to live a life different from her mother's. And so she rejected Massimo's advances, though she liked him well enough, and became engaged to Sergio, who expected to study engineering thanks to his father's savings. No sooner was she betrothed however than Sergio intensified their encounters in a remote cabin, following which they had to get married — fast. One thing led to another and his father's savings were spent on grappa, and in the end Sergio bought a boat from a retired fisherman and christened it with the name of his wife. While he spent part of his nights on the lake, Anna Maria's beautiful hands were busy changing diapers. Then, after fifteen years of fried fish and boredom, she grew stout, lost a few teeth, and bought cotton underwear. You don't rechristen a boat. As far as Sergio was concerned, the

blue *Anna Maria* transported to the middle of the lake his wife's
bad moods and her reproaches as to the quality of the fish,
the profession of fisherman, her children's bad grades, and
life in general. In the eyes of Massimo, who'd never married,
the red *Anna Maria* still played operatic arias, he could hear
it on the water just before dawn, and when he bent over her
side to straighten his nets, his reflection could see beautiful
hands coming out the window between two clothespins.

From the harbour, in exchange for a considerable sum,
tourists set sail for the Blue Island. In the Middle Ages the
island had belonged to a prince who offered it as a gift to the
pope. Monks lived there, perhaps some prisoners too. Now
it's owned by an American. On the south coast, a natural
stairway in the rock descends ceremoniously into the water.
The island is streaked with paths that cross the forest, opening now and then onto a clearing, an ancient field cultivated
by the monks. It has nine chapels in more or less good shape.
In one of them can still be seen remains of a fresco executed
by a well-known artist whose name the tourist guide always
forgets. Another chapel stands balanced on the cliff from
where the monks would attack with slingshots any fishermen
who violated the territory of the Church. An unusual hole
one metre wide and ten deep — dungeon or observatory —
adds to the mystery of the site. The sky is wide, the water
crystal-clear, tourists leave the island already missing it, and
as the boat moves away, they watch it sparkle — peaceful,
eternal.

They go back to the harbour. In the harbour, objects move and people walk. By day and by night the pulleys beat an unsettled rhythm on the masts. A cement wharf juts into the water and branches off at a right angle, hugging the boats to protect them from the waves. From the end of the wharf only the lake can be seen and, rarely, the other shore. You can make out the silhouette of the Blue Island — asymmetrical, like a cake that's fallen on the left, similar also to the snake swallowing an elephant on the first page of *The Little Prince*. On the left, a little farther away, emerge the humps of its four sisters, among them the one from where, one stormy day, Marco's grandfather abducted his grandmother.

Near the wharf there are stands overflowing with souvenirs, each more morbid than the others: Etruscan key rings, Etruscan ashtrays, plastic vases, plastic fruit, plastic popes, plastic pottery. A public telephone displays an "out of service" sign, a clock shows eleven o'clock for all eternity, and no one minds because twice a day, it does show the right time.

Besides, time is different. It's in the way they all move, catlike, reserving their sustained attention for a possible encounter, as if walking were neither an activity in itself nor a means of getting from one point to another, but rather the creation of a public space, a lure for coincidence. As if people only walk to stop at any moment. They walk or they drive around the block. They look around in case they might recognize someone. They recognize someone: they stop. Nothing else matters. Time is elastic, there's always room in it for a coffee, sure, why not, a good coffee. The place where they're going can wait, because they're needed in the place where they are now. They chat. While they chat, they lock eyes firmly with the other, place a hand on his arm. With excessive gesticulation, they import the entire universe into the limited circle of their narrative — because in the end they rarely say anything that sticks. They smile. Their smile comes straight from childhood, passing through a zone of shadow during adolescence, which claims to be above everything but that reappears eventually — intact, more and more childlike as age takes back the necessary modesty. A smile stripped of any agenda, in the space of which objective time broadens out: even if they stop they'll never be late, because being late is part of being punctual, richness is proportionate to slowness. And anyway, if administrations worked as well as coffee machines, it wouldn't be exactly their country anymore.

This village still exists, as it is, at this very moment.

After the harbour, the promenade continues along the lake. Pine trees alternate with willows here and there. Between restaurants and campgrounds there are gardens where, on some nights in June, foam snows onto round grass, green stars, mature flowers. Night falls softly, attracted to the ground by their frail fingers. On the terraces the setting sun flickers in the metallic lacework of chairs and tables, glasses and utensils flow, transparent as water, onto a display window.

One terrace, set back, with pink tablecloths and plastic chairs, belongs to a modest café where they make a revolting cappuccino, and where very early one morning, Marianne saw the waitress crying between willows that suddenly resembled her distraught face.

The promenade ends at a second, wider beach that all summer is littered with burned flesh, children's shouts and beach balls, sputtering radios, the smell of almond and coconut, towels, parasols, cartons of cigarettes, snatches of conversations in all the languages of Europe, dominated always by German. On the hottest days, the beach spills over into the lake. There are so many swimmers, the water turns cloudy. Even if you swim with your eyes open, you make out other bodies only by bumping into them, and some moustachioed males take advantage of it, rubbing up against the blondest teenage girls. Between May and September the only time to find peace and quiet is before eight in the morning, in the company of two or three retired Englishmen with very white ankles.

The road ends at a traffic circle, conveniently for some nonchalant drivers who come there to watch the girls swim, their windows all rolled down. They travel at three kilometres an hour, turn back onto the road from the traffic circle, driving past the beach again and then into a hotel parking lot; they wait a while, then drive around again until a girl comes out of the water. Then they park, get out of their cars, and in a version of English that sounds like Romanian, they hold out a card that turns them into doctors or optometrists, invite her for a drink, *"perchè no?"* for dinner, *"you see I have car, I can outside of village take you."* To which the girl, tangled up in her towel that's suddenly too short, manages to murmur, *"no, grazie,"* and they compliment her effusively on her command of Italian, *"how you learn so good?"* To which, sure that she is thereby putting a final stop to the conversation, she claims that there's already a man in her life, and they step up their efforts. But a firm rejection is enough for their attitude to change. As they've done with girls on other days, they level a smile at her which shows that, in spite of everything, they're pleased; they say goodbye and leave to resume their patrol, giving the impression that the purpose of the game was merely to formulate the invitation, to practise the innocent art of being virile according to principles internalized since childhood, like repeating a prayer learned by heart, bereft of content but whose strung-together syllables possess a kind of authority. In fact they'd have been upset if she had accepted, because then they'd have had to lie to wives or mothers, had to spend money, and make an extra effort to speak English.

Behind the beach, a path runs into a clump of rushes bent over at the most vulnerable point on their stems. The packed sand stretches out, damp, onto the grass-covered slope. The sun drops in shreds. Humidity wraps everything in an extreme green. Footsteps crush stems and the planks of rotten wood flung onto the less negotiable parts. On the left, an endless fence protects the gardens of the lakeside residents, gardens that boldly reveal their owners' character — by means of lawn chairs, hammocks, bottles no longer virgin, and lanterns; or lawns that are neglected but fertile; or tables set in the open air with faded cloths; or yellowed newspapers, cups, ashtrays, children's toys, sailboards, open windows, closed windows, barred windows. On the right, the rushes open onto private beaches, and behind them the lake — vast, bright, misty, choppy, flat. Abandoned boats, other chairs, beach balls: as if for some people the gardens had jumped the fence to come and sit by the water. On the beaches people raise ducks, build open structures that the vegetation carefully finishes off; party leftovers are abandoned to age there, debris of happy days spent listening to the water flow; they make a dock from which to dive or embark on a sailboard, postponing the moment of getting wet. These are the estates of the poor, anonymous kingdoms protected by a padlock on some chicken wire.

Marianne often walks along the corridor of rushes. She peers at the gardens like someone attending a ball through a window. While others are off at work in the daylight, she examines closely the remains of their Sundays and of their summer nights. She does her best to understand, to get used to these lives as to a giddy spell, lives that, if she wanted, could become hers too. She imagines these lives settled into the gardens, guesses the women's weight from the strain on the chairs, the men's mood from how well the lawns are kept up. It's easy to see that there's no winter. The December rains aren't much more taxing than the blazing sun. Dozens of generations of eroded objects lie scattered in the sand; chair legs point to utensils that would delight archaeologists; time passes nonchalantly, women, men are born, love one another, hate one another, die — and the faithful objects still lie, indifferent, lazy beneath the sky.

I feel dizzy at the thought that this village still exists, with the moon slung across its serene sky, and that at this very moment, I'm certain, the island is concocting a miracle in the tiny shade of its nine chapels.

I wanted to know everything about you. To crack open your timid heart like a nut and feel its liberated sunlight spread over me.

My first room in the deserted hotel was a big one, with a high ceiling and two vast windows. Through one of them I could see the village squeezed between the walls that leave one tower of the castle visible. Through the other, a whole branch of the chestnut tree in blossom came in, and if I leaned out, I could often see the peculiar statue of Christ that was missing a hand. I met you that way. My room opened onto your country through two unshuttered eyes, and Christ was missing a hand.

I know that it's impossible to live two lives at once. I entered your country after giving up on it in advance, but still I was eager, still I expected all of it — your sky, its storm, your violent solitude, the barking of your dogs: I wanted everything. I left everything behind, like a puddle of rainwater, like a soiled sheet, like the remains of dinner on the counter, I abandoned it all when I left, just as it was, there, at your place, and you, I simply allowed you to be. There is only one life, only one, and I let you cut into it with another possible life, a life for the two of us that must be extinguished now, slowly, while I melt back into the snow to which I was promised.

There was an empty seat next to mine on the plane, it was surely the void that sat down there. It deplaned with me, went through customs, claimed its baggage, appropriated the free space in my house; it wakes me in the morning by pressing on the pillow, it slips between my hand and the objects of my life. It is the last trial between us and it may be the hardest, the most painful, the longest of our moments together; it's waiting until I stop missing you before it sneaks away, until I stop trembling when I've dreamed about you, until I stop being silent when my friends ask me questions; it is waiting with me, side-by-side, for winter to be over, and then the year; together, we're waiting for me to stop waiting.

The village still exists, and its image attacks me by surprise, at any hour of the night or day. When I'm reading the bilingual label on a box of cereal, when I'm shovelling the stairs, when I'm making photocopies on both sides of the paper for my boss, and when my godson falls asleep in my arms. Everything is a madeleine for me and my involuntary memory is activated against my will, perhaps so I won't lose you absolutely, perhaps so I won't completely lose what I was at that time.

Over there, there was so little horizon.

II

TO BE NOTHING BUT A DOG

*S*ometimes when Marco was a child, his mother would look for him when she got up in the morning. He wasn't in the house, he wasn't in the garden. Eventually she would find him lying in his German shepherd's kennel. They slept together in the combined and peaceful warmth of animal and child.

Marco only adopts dogs whose birth he has witnessed. Peggy has given him two litters from which he adopted first Fulli, sole survivor of a virus, and a few years afterwards Ambra and Argo. When Marianne enters their family story, Peggy is old and mangy with lumps deforming her cancer-riddled body. Marco repeats that she's had her golden age, that she's been beautiful, agile, brilliant, that she was loyal. She is the queen and always will be. She sleeps in his room and the two of them share abiding memories of hunting and games. If he exaggerates when he tells the story, she is silent in sympathy so as not to spoil his pleasure.

One autumn day, Marco reluctantly moves Peggy into the cubbyhole with the water heater. These are her final days, he and his mother both know that, but they don't talk about it because they never talk. About anything. The vet arrives with his syringe. He stabs her hide, Marco turns around, crosses his arms, and tries to focus on his tax return. Every day that follows, every day in his life, he will add baroque gold ornamentation when he talks about her, and when he repeats the story of the three trips he's taken (Sardinia, Sicily, Calabria), he never leaves out the fact that she was there too, and when he talks about mushrooms, he never forgets to mention that they hunted together, and when he talks about hunting, he'll most certainly add that she could track an enormous pheasant even after the rain had wiped out any sign of its trail. The cubbyhole still smells like her, like an old dog. "Nobody but me can smell it, I don't want to clean it. Maybe I should have watched her die, I should have petted her. Maybe she thought I was abandoning her."

After Peggy's death, Fulli is promoted to the top of the hierarchy. He moves elegantly, with the stillness of an ambassador, and he has an aristocratic way of holding his head. He never barks except for some serious reason. He observes wisely and he understands every word. When he doesn't obey, it's because his master is in the wrong. And yet he always carries a kind of sadness. Marco suspects that he knows he was chosen not for himself but because all his brothers and sisters were killed by the virus. "No one," he says, "can live in peace with a thought like that, Fulli can't any more than anyone else."

Argo and Ambra are twins. He is timid and clumsy, she's lively and delinquent. They disobey constantly, he from obtuseness, she from intelligence. Ambra often gets hurt and because of her, Marco spends all his spare time with the homeopathic veterinarian who rarely gets paid, because Marco is his best client: aside from the dogs, he also entrusts both himself and his mother to him.

Leaving the vet's office on the night when Ambra gets a splinter the size of a nail in her paw, Marco takes a rough dirt path — the kind he likes. He stops in the forest, opens the door: Fulli gets out with style, Argo follows. Ambra stays in the Jeep and gives him a pleading look. "Come on, Ambra, get out." She moans. "Come on, Ambra," he repeats, changing his tone, "I'm here, I'll help you, come on, I'm right here." He bends down and still talking, draws her to him and picks her up. "Come on, I'm here." She's heavy. He sets her on the ground and Ambra starts walking and crying. Marco squats down and covers her with his whole body, he tightens his arms around her chest and rubs his cheek against her head. He rocks her. For a long time he rocks her, talking to her in hushed tones. Marianne watches them from a distance: she knows that he'll never love humans the way he loves dogs, devoted to their straw bodies, steeped in their loyalty.

One morning a few months later, Ambra dies on the floor of the garage, after three cruel days of writhing in pain and one last night of howling while everyone was asleep. He buries her next to Peggy, in the place where he raises his ducks, determined never to resign himself to that task. She was too young, too full of life, with her beautiful, finely sculpted muzzle and her oh-so-feminine way of disobeying him; he doesn't understand. "There are all kinds of dogs on the street that are hungry, sad, alone, and those dogs will live to a hundred, while mine are dropping like leaves in the first gust of wind."

From then on he displays an outraged sorrow. He caresses in a new way, eyes closed, with a delicacy as soft as flour and Marianne understands that it's the death of the dogs that's shivering in the tips of his fingers, she understands that their interrupted race will pass through all his gestures yet to come.

You may be poor, as poor as I am, as devoid of a country, as devoid of patience. I've seen you suffer, but in the way a stone would suffer: silently and with no danger of breaking. Without tears. Without panic. You suffer quietly, without dismembering north from south, east, west. You suffer methodically, putting evil on one side, good on the other, and listing the ambiguous in the column of things to review, tomorrow. I loved your suffering as much as your happiness, maybe even more, maybe I only loved your happiness when it progressed beyond your suffering. I loved the way your hand settled onto objects, with no hesitation, appropriating them for as long as necessary, then letting them go naturally back to themselves. In the same way you took my body and gave it back to me.

Loving you meant agreeing to leave you alone, to being alone beside you, and it was knowing that always you would leave at five a.m., whether or not there was a woman in your bed. Not to be responsible for anyone is the way you've chosen to be responsible for yourself. It's an ascetic selfishness. Your solitude is regal, you don't commit yourself with words. Sometimes you forgive, but you never ask forgiveness. You are grandiose but separate from the rest of men and from whatever it is in you that needs to know them. You don't know anyone. No one knows you. Except your dogs. Except the echo of the November rifle.

Hunters hunt because it's the most adventurous activity they can find on territory civilized earlier by the Etruscans, conquered by the Romans, broken by Fascism, bogged down in shady policies. As for natural enemies, the only ones left are some pheasants, some ducks, and the odd wild boar.

Hunting does create another enemy though, one that's more dangerous, more cunning: the other hunter. Because the territory is limited, the other hunter is always too close, and while the urge might be there, you can't shoot him. Instead you must try to avoid him. The most hardened, like Marco, choose to set out very early, to hunt on weekdays or under unpleasant conditions (rain, cold, mud). As for the more sedentary, they start a rumour that two boar and a whole family of pheasants have been spotted in the third copse on the right at the back of Giuseppe Marconi's field, or that there's nothing interesting behind Luisa's vineyard. Those hunters recognize each other by the time they choose to visit the central bar and by the powerful voice they take on to address the biggest audience possible. Generally they're the same ones you notice furtively stuffing the trunks of their cars with more woodcocks than the legal limit and on that same night, denying that they've shot anything at all.

A number of them exhibit a wealth of imagination for unearthing the ideal spot for a blind (two planks, two beams, a cardboard roof) to hunt ducks from between the reeds that grow next to the lake. It has to be a strategic place for migration: while the best situated will have at their disposal a complete V of ducks, the others will see at most a sentence written in Braille. But it's not just a question of appropriating the best location for themselves, they must protect it too. Anything can happen: fires, threats — misspelled and anonymous — theft of roof or floor. Plots are many, and enemies relentless.

That's why the law gets involved in hunting problems — as in all other problems for that matter. The law in this country is the art of nabbing those who have the skill to get around it. The essence of the law lies in its inevitable failure, and as a result, it reproduces like a litter of rabbits, it divides, becomes more specific, at times contradicts itself; it takes on encyclopedic dimensions which confirm to the citizen that obedience is impossible.

There is a limit to the number of rifles a family is allowed to own. The power of the shot is subject to inspection. You must fire towards the sky, never towards the ground. Tuesdays and Fridays are days of rest for the dogs. It's forbidden to buy or sell devices that imitate the cries of the desired species, but there are some who record the sound of their domesticated ducks — or that of a particularly gifted grandfather. The hunters can't cross the regional boundary that is marked, depending on the place, by a rope, a sign, a stream, or a hill. Trained from earliest childhood to recognize the boundary, they can't make a mistake. The difficulty of complying with the regulation though is immense. What is more frustrating than to see the pheasant you've pursued from copse to copse suddenly reappear on the forbidden side of the stream with the text of the law tucked under its wing? How can you explain to your dogs that you have to give up the pursuit, how can you overcome their disconsolate look? One day or another most hunters have seen the prey cross the legal boundary. Reactions to this trauma are varied. Some choose to laugh at the law, others ignore it, others come to doubt the existence of God. And others still make up cathartic tales in which the goddamn pheasant becomes more and more beautiful, more and more plump, even becomes, sometimes, a whole family of pheasants — or even a boar.

The crux of the problem and the principal reason for hostility has to do with the shortage of wild animals. To compensate for it, some associations undertake every summer to raise pheasants in the hundreds and release them a few weeks before the hunting season opens, crossing their fingers that the birds will respect the border and that they'll survive being out in the wild.

Over the course of the weeks before the season opens, the hunters get used to their uniforms again. They seem to come straight out of war footage as they stroll around in khaki and leather boots, artfully camouflaging themselves with beards that look like the dry bushes in the undergrowth. They make their dogs walk for an hour or two every day, testing their muscles, increasing their protein intake. They conspire against one another, form teams, and cook up strategies so that no beginner will come and spoil the long-awaited day. The closer it comes, the harder it is for them to concentrate on anything else.

The hunting season opens gradually. First turtledoves; then ducks, later on pheasants, woodcocks, quail, pigeons, and boar. Most animals perish on the first day. Three hens and a farmer are hit by mistake. The rest of the season is just a bland series of disappointments, of hours spent with ears pricked at the sound of one's own boots, bawling out the dogs who end up playing among themselves. Conversations, briefly devoted to reckoning the take, move on to the problem of the shortage of animals, and stretch out more and more often over a cappuccino. Those who'd managed to get up at four a.m. in late September get up at nine in mid-October, and by the beginning of December, keep the hunt for Sunday afternoons. They go back to anticipating the opening next season, convincing themselves that it was better last year, muttering that so-and-so exceeded the quota, that the fields are too open, the woods too sparse.

And so the winter days are filled. With rifles loaded and pants soaked in mud, each man wants to know how many animals his neighbour took, in which copse, on which road; each one thinks that his dog is the best and he'd sell his soul to see his photo in the national hunting magazine. Despite the meagre take from their favourite sport, they're no doubt happy to feel their seven-league boots advance; to carry deferentially in their frozen hands the metal butt of a rifle they'll set down on the stroke of one, next to the table where most certainly awaits the pasta prepared by their mother, who's a better cook than all the others. No doubt they're happy that around the restricted geography of the genuine territory stretches the infinite expanse of their conversations, for in fact their true territory is nothing but a fantasy.

Marco devotes most of his time to getting ready for the hunt. When he can't sleep, he makes his own cartridges. With cold, rhythmical, hypnotic movements he weighs the lead shot on an ancient scale, pours it into an orange tube for the most potent cartridges, red for those the law allows, and a few inconsequential blue ones for Marianne to practise shooting with — one of these days. On some long rainy afternoons he sets himself up in his garage and meticulously paints the breasts of the plastic ducks, taking as model the photos in the hunting magazine he subscribes to. On a former fish-farming site that belongs to his cousin he has built a paradise for raising domesticated ducks. Once the eggs hatch, he brings the babies home where he can look after them and keep them warm. He puts them in a shoebox which he opens ten times during the journey to check if they've moved and if they're happy. The duck is his favourite animal because, he says, "It looks so beautiful when it flies."

On duck-hunting days he gets up at three a.m. — meaning that he doesn't sleep at all. He attaches a weight to the feet of the tame ducks to keep them from flying away. Then he goes to the back of his cousin's house, frees his boat from the tall grass where it's hidden, and pushes his way through the water to his blind. He stands to manoeuvre the boat because of the local oars, which are longer than the rower is tall, each arm executing a movement opposite to the other. Once he's arrived, he arranges the birds — real and fake — on the lake, experimenting with a different layout of his fleet each time, methodically empirical. He works the way an artist would work on an ephemeral installation that only he will have the time to gaze at: he and the wild birds. Occasionally, he observes ducks that he thinks are his until they fly off, before he's had time to shoot, caught in his own trap and perfectly content.

If he decides to go into the woods, he gets up around five, pulls on wool socks, heavy boots, a flannel shirt, a tight T-shirt, and pants with all kinds of pockets. Rifle and ammunition are already in the Jeep. He takes a paper bag from the fridge, which his mother has filled with bread, cheese, and apples.

He loads the dogs into his vehicle, starts it up, drives for a long time. He likes the ritual of surrounding himself with the same objects, leaving at an excessively early hour, travelling far, being alone: he loves hunting. He thinks about his father who, having only five bullets at his disposal, walked all the way to Grado to hunt. He thinks about his passion for hunting, the passion they share. It's as if he were going to meet him and when he shoots with the same legendary precision, he feels his father's approval from on high. He enjoys these hours when he talks only to the dogs, these hours when his dogs answer him, these hours similar to those he spent as a child, sleeping in the dog's kennel. What he likes most of all is the possibility of being a dog.

He's fired up if his squad stops, tails wagging, at the entrance to a woods, detecting the animal's presence. He thinks. Depending on humidity, the direction of the wind, the presence of a stream, depending on the kind of vegetation, on whether or not he's seen feathers stuck on thorns or tracks on the ground, depending on his own hunting memories, and his father's, and those of other hunters, which are stacked up inside him like the volumes of a living encyclopaedia, he works out his strategy and decides if he'll go into the woods. For him, hunting is a game of chess, he enjoys losing as much as winning, and he lives with the illusion that his prey is as intelligent as a Russian champion. The animals he kills are animals he has first talked to. He finds them, loses them, recognizes them, waits for them. One pheasant keeps him on tenterhooks for an entire season. Marco curses it, but is secretly proud to have found an adversary able to shake him off.

The bird falls and the dogs retrieve it. He holds it in his open hand, looks at it, strokes its beak and feathers, locates the holes left by the shot, then drops it into his bag with the indifference he often displays for things from the past. He kills as many animals as he can eat. He opens his freezer and counts the remains; when he concludes that *basta adesso*, he turns in his rifle for a camera.

The dealings of his dogs among themselves fascinate him. He feeds them better than princes, trains them, sticks under their muzzles pheasant feathers and the meat that his mother is preparing to cook. He always takes along a young dog and an older one. He marvels at the sight of the older one setting an example for the younger and the younger learning, disobeying, trying out a new manoeuvre, understanding that he was wrong, and trying to get Marco's approval all the same.

"Peggy was a perfect mother. One day, for instance, when two birds had fallen, now listen carefully, *due uccelli in una volta sola*, she tore into the water to get the one that had fallen the farthest, checking from the corner of her eye that Fulli could get the other one so he'd have a little success of his own. Argo is still young, take a good look, watch him watching Fulli and hoping he'll surpass him in the hierarchy. He tries to bite him now and then, but Fulli only sneers. Each of them gets his turn, *è così vero?* One day Fulli will be old and Argo will be the strongest. If I can find a female for Fulli she'll have puppies, I'd like another girl, so it's Argo who would show her everything. But before that, he has to learn, and he's so impatient, *madonna mia!* that dog is so impatient, he's the most impatient of them all, and a little bit clumsy on top of it, isn't he, *che ci posso fare io*, what can I do? *Niente! Aspetto*, I wait."

He hunts until it's time to go to work. His clothes are wet, he's cold when he stops and too hot when he walks, his bag is heavy, his rifle is heavy, the fields slope and the woods are full of thorns. He also enjoys feeling tired, the holes in his clothes from the branches, the sweat that soaks the prickly wool, he enjoys the way the dogs run in an ellipse, the colour of the rain, the Jeep's drive wheels, the dry shoes he puts on before getting back on the road, the imperceptible changes in the spots he's been going to since childhood. He enjoys the absence of humans; now and then he'll pick up a pebble.

After supper, around nine o'clock in the evening, he sits by the fireplace where his mud-encrusted boots are drying. He throws on a log, listens to the fire and falls fast asleep almost at once, until his own snoring wakes him up; then he drags himself to his bed, sometimes gets undressed, sometimes sleeps with all his clothes on.

The next day he wakes up around five. The rifle, the ammunition, and the dogs are ready, and the damp night encircles them like friendly arms they happily step into — and it's the same every day.

Some people are incapable of talking in a low voice. You, though, can project your voice and put on a show, and you also know how to reduce it to an essential thread, to a minimal sound in the dimness of bedrooms.

You taught me, I think, how to hear and see. By observing the back of your neck I understood how to draw windows, streets, chairs, tables. My hearing, my eyesight, have no object now. I'm trying to find a world for them. I'm waiting until, in the absence of your neck, the windows and streets, the chairs, tables reappear, with the remarkable smile they wear when someone gets ready to see them. I think of you alive, up since five a.m., laughing at your own mistakes, with the dust that rolls around in the tramontana. I want to exist the way you exist, with the pride that has made me suffer so much, but from which I know that you'll die on your feet. The space is still between us, it keeps us at arm's length, and what you've put inside me I must carry and care for, like a difficult child.

You didn't cry when I flew away.

You asked me not to cry. I stole your image, I had less than a minute. To fly was the only thing I could do on that day and by flying resemble the most beautiful animal.

III

THE ALL-ROUND MOTHER

$\mathcal{M}$arianne goes for weeks without meeting Marco's mother. She can't imagine her as anything but a gaping hole that swallows him up at certain precise times: mealtimes, to which she's not yet welcome. The mother is well aware that her son doesn't sleep at home now, but she asks no questions for fear of finding out what she already knows through the aunt: another foreigner. Marco grants her the favour of his presence by day and takes it away for the night. In this way he divides himself between mother and lover until, tired of all these comings and goings, he finally makes up his mind.

When Marianne steps inside Marco's house for the first time, the mother goes to the doorstep and vigorously shakes her hand. Before Marianne has time to open her mouth, she has already turned her back, her hands are already in the sink washing the vegetables.

There is sand in her voice and a certain harshness which shows that she's not just a mother, she's a field marshal, with weapons that smell good at mealtimes and a regiment of pots and pans under her command. Her excellent cooking is renowned throughout the village. Restaurants have tried to hire her, she's always said no, her art is reserved for her men. She pours oil onto the lettuce, holding the huge bottle in one hand, thumb over the opening to control the flow. She cuts bread like a cowboy, pushing the knife towards herself. She works with superfluous movements that look scientific. She realized long ago that she holds onto her men by the stomach, which compensates entirely for the fact that they keep her in the kitchen.

Her age is impossible to guess. Short, bouncy, white hair, she says things that make her laugh and she says rude things, things like the ones that little girls tell one another. She also does things that wound, as when after supper one evening, seeing that Marianne is clearing the table, shaking the table-cloth out the window, folding it carefully and putting it away in a drawer, she takes it out, snaps it open, folds it again, and puts it away. In the same drawer.

When she prepares the birds Marco has shot, she starts by cutting off the head and feet, then she plucks them.

She takes out the entrails and stuffs the birds with a mix-ture of olives and bread, then she sews up the stomachs as conscientiously as she darns socks or crochets lace. Preparing the birds takes all afternoon, it's the final stage of Marco's work, of his work of art that began on the lake or on the scale where he weighs the lead shot. She puts into cooking all her respect for her son and through it, all his respect for the animals, and through that, their shared respect for life.

Her culinary knowledge is at once luminous and obscure. Degree zero of the recipe: *minestra* — water, vegetables, beans, rice; tomato salad — tomatoes, oil, salt; yet elaborate dishes end up on the table. On the first days, she lapses into the gargantuan, both at noon and at night. Pasta, two meat dishes, fried vegetables, salad, cheese, tart, fruit: it's to welcome Marianne nicely, perhaps, or to act in such a way that she has nothing to find fault with because everything is known. It may be to please Marco by making him aware that she's delighted there's finally a woman in his life, or maybe to obey him — she can't refuse him anything. Maybe it's to seduce Marianne into staying as long as possible rather than taking Marco to some other continent, or maybe it's to paralyze her, take away her ability to feed herself, tie her to her plate and give her a round belly that would make her unable to talk, to get up, to go away. Marianne will never really know. What *is* known for certain is that with her short, firm hands the mother loads her plate without asking any questions, without trying to find out who she is, what she wants, how long she intends to stay in the empty house. A week later, with many exclamations, Marco begs his mother to curb her enthusiasm. "I'll get fat, I'll explode, Marianne will explode, we'll all explode."

Marianne eats well, she has always eaten well. It's not enough. *"Mangia, mangia,"* says the mother before she has even finished what's on her plate. "Thank you, *grazie,*" Marianne refuses with the obligatory politeness and a movement of her hand, "really."

"Ma dai, mangia," insists the mother and at that point in the dialogue, the same point every time, she tosses a piece of meat on her plate or pours onto it the contents of the frying pan. At first, Marianne is amused by her insistence, flattered too. Then it starts to get on her nerves. She says "no more" brusquely, considers not eating what is forced on her, but she's reluctant to leave it. Finally, Marco intervenes: *"Mamma,"* he says, "she's big enough to make up her own mind. Stop." Which is still not enough and the next day, when a pork chop lands heavily on her plate, Marianne, exasperated, transfers it to Marco's. Without a word, but without appetite either, he eats it. The scene is repeated the following days: *Mangia, mangia*, no, thank you, it was very good, really, shower of tomatoes, transfer to Marco's plate, his sighs, the sound of his fork, *mangia*, chicken breast, *grazie*, *no*, piece of sausage, prosciutto, apple, pear, fig. It all ends up with Marco, who is starting to show signs of distress.

Mute signals, no more than an exhausted look at his mother, the sketch of an impatient gesture, hardly anything. But finally, she has understood. This is about her son. Her son, whose limits she knows and submits to as to the Ten Commandments. No more negotiating. Marianne has won because Marco has won. If she wants more meat, she helps herself. When she's eaten her fill, she takes nothing more. Her white plate stays white and her liver, intact.

The table is the altar of an untouchable life in which the foreigner has suddenly appeared, like a hair in the *minestra*, like one mouth too many between child and breast. Because in fact the distance between Marco and his mother is no larger than the table, and the table isn't a real distance, it's their most tangible connection, their common language, under the tablecloth is an invisible love letter and on top of it, the mother sets down plates that twice a day, miraculously, transform her son into a punctual man.

A mother is a mother in most cases. Her diffuse power branches out in songs, in knowing how to make and do everything — a fire, coffee; and in knowing how to listen, to guess, to console; to buy soap, cheese; to find the missing shoelace in a corner of the cupboard or the right word, the one word out of all others, all the words of others, that will guarantee unconditional love.

At the age when he still submits to his mother's voice, the child is not yet aware of the brutal fact that elsewhere, around that voice and outside it, there is an indifferent universe, streaked with stray arrows waiting for his inexperienced body, waiting for his naïveté that's offered prematurely and with no ulterior motive; the child is ignorant of the nature of exchanges and of the cruel and arid duty that will be imposed on him as soon as he starts school. But it is from the world itself, cruel as it is, that the child will learn that there's no absolute, that there are only other elsewheres. He will grow up and step into ingratitude, as if the milk of happiness were turning sour. Some mothers agree to give up their kingdom, they lay their burden down on the earth and open wide the door, mourning no doubt, but in agreement. They're still available and have within easy reach a medicine chest that can take care of everything. The return home of an injured child is a celebration, a sad, short celebration, unmention-able, camouflaged behind the accessibility of an attentive ear, and some mothers even go so far as to become friends.

In political terms, Marco's country belongs to a handful of citizens, but it's also the country of everyone, it is said to be the cradle of western civilization, it is the mother's voice gently seizing the world to make it fit to live in, soothing with the palm of her hand the very first suspicion, smoothing into the child's hair an opaque lullaby that often keeps him from growing, holding him in her arms until he suffocates. In that country, motherhood has such power that it transcends in power education, government, the Church. The mother is Mary, already a victim of the wicked who will take away her son. To give is her vocation. By giving, the mother is the Madonna and she cannot be abandoned.

In the mediocre, magnificent village, its belly held tight

by its belt of stone, Marco's mother married a childhood friend, a fisherman like half the men in the village, like his father and his grandfather before him. She was young and very beautiful, with plump cheeks, perfect teeth, and eyes like black pearls. Her husband was honest, hard-working, quick-tempered, depressive. His skin was warm, his forehead high. They had no ambition beyond finding their place in the village, submitting to the atavistic rhythm of established rules, and not disturbing anything in that microcosm. They went out together on the boat every night, taking the nets she crocheted. When they came back in the morning, she washed the fish, filleted it, and sold it. Very soon, they had a son and six years later, a second. She never slept, except when her body collapsed like a bundle in the boat or in some Etruscan's open grave. She said little. She did. Did the things that had to be done and did them perfectly. She observed her older son and her husband carry on a furious battle that wouldn't end until the older man died — and not even then, really. She took refuge in the growth of the younger son, Marco, the child who was seven before he talked, who slept in the dogs' kennel and rarely played the same games as others. Year after year, she repeated actions learned from her mother and from all the mothers before her — cutting the bread and tomatoes, pouring oil onto them, making coffee before someone asked, before they even realized they wanted it, ironing sheets till they were as smooth and white as the paper of those who know how to write. She became expert at these actions, she became the irreplaceable head of the family, making ends meet and giving her husband just enough to drink away his depression.

She became Action. Even today, all her energy goes into it, and all her person and all the meaning of life, and when there's nothing left to knit for her family, she knits bonnets for the children of others.

The first son is gone. The husband is dead. Marco is still at home, shut up in his silence and in his remarkable gaze. He is the Kingdom, he is Life, the things done for him are the only ones possible, they're the eternal actions, the ones without which the sky would be empty. The stagnant centuries of the village have stolen from the mother any other form of identity. Her last son is stamped onto her skin like the print of a fossil; their separation is inconceivable.

She warns Marianne as soon as they're alone for the first time: "Marco will never leave, you know; he told me so, he said it like this, now listen, he said: I'll never leave." Marianne knows that Marco is incapable of making such a promise, she also knows that it doesn't matter, that those words his mother has put in his mouth have a power of truth that surpasses everything else, that surpasses reality itself. She knows that she'll have to struggle against them and she knows that she'll lose the battle. Each day spent in Marco's country is a day spent losing him, a day spent accepting that he shrinks back behind his mother's mouth, behind the wall of the village.

You run to the car in the rain. We count the ducks between the rushes, you see five, I see six, mysteriously they disappear. I've put a long table in my house to make room for disorder, any kind of disorder. Your country rises, fateful, along my throat, it extends its hand. While I'm swimming in the lake, you walk along the shore, carrying my clothes on a stick. You hold out your hand that's filled with figs and hazelnuts, I see it that way between two breaststrokes, diagonal and full in the mauve line of the evening. I think about the roads in your country and on both sides the wind, the sunflowers that tell the time, the yellow sky above them. I hear the roads. They chatter and they hold me in a terrible emptiness, they steal what's left to me here — the grocery list, the schedule for the bus that takes me to the centre of town.

Idle, Marianne tries to find some innocent activity. After a moment, she thinks about the garden in front of the empty house. Marco's mother sowed some seeds there so she'd have a fresh stock of flowers to take every day to her husband's grave. The flowers are already high, they sparkle, but weeds have grown too and when she notices them, Marianne thinks, That's it, perfect. With the sun like a brick on her shoulders, she starts weeding. What she knows about gardening is truly appalling, but no one will see, once the weeds have been put in the garbage, that she has also included a few of what might have been flowers. Less and less scrupulous, more and more merciless, she leaves her mark on the garden, happily frenzied in this major cleaning job.

When she hears Marco's mother's bicycle come around the corner, her blood runs cold. She jumps up and stands in front of the pile of weeds, hoping without much confidence that it won't be noticed. But the mother knows. Faster than her shadow, she rushes at Marianne, pushes her with one hand, takes one look at the pile of weeds, another look at the garden, then rolls both eyes to heaven. It hasn't taken her five seconds to assess the situation and her diagnosis is clear: this is a case of garden murder.

"I could beat you, what are you doing, I plant flowers and you pull them up, a garden's not supposed to be weeded anyway! Ah! *Madonna mia, ma che hai fatto!*"

Seething with exclamations, beside herself, and with no respect for the fine clothes she wears for visiting the cemetery, she kneels, takes from the pile of weeds those that would turn into flowers, and puts them back in the ground, *ma veramente*, waters them, floods them, violently pounds the soil around them, *mamma mia*, while Marianne, rigid with shame, tries in vain to blend with the whitewash on the house. The mother finishes her repairs, shoots a furious look at her, and stomps out of the garden, her Mass shoes covered with mud.

Starting that day, Marianne begins to suffer from having to detest something as beautiful and fragile as the flutter of a red petal against the blue of evening when it's windy, even just a little. But she can't help it: the longest flower stems are as upright as the bars of a cage.

I have put the immense table in one room of my house, so that some disorder could expand — mine.

Often she asks her for recipes. Like all experienced cooks, Marco's mother never knows what to reply.

"You have to pluck the bird, chop off the head, cut it up, stuff it with a mixture of olives and breadcrumbs and oil and spices."

"Which spices?"

"Oh, well, that depends on what you've got."

"And why is the *minestra* so thick?"

"Why? Because it's thick."

"And the fresh pasta?"

"What, you don't know how to make your own pasta?" (Surprised, slightly condescending.) "Come early some night and watch me."

According to the cook, the ingredients are always the same, the preparation is always the same, yet the meal is always different. Several times, Marianne comes to watch, but she doesn't really learn anything that might be useful later; all she learns is the curve drawn by hands that do everything quickly and well, all she learns is the route taken by footsteps in the big kitchen, everywhere at once — to the oven, the table, the sink. It's hot, the gas flame adds to the sweltering heat, and the mother never sweats.

Her isolation, her meagre knowledge of the language, and her own idleness confer on Marianne more and more the identity of a slug. Every mouthful she ingests at Marco's mother's table reinforces that image, she knows it, and as the weeks go by she reaches the point where she'd give anything to be able to offer some dazzling proof of her normality, like those frogs that turn into princes.

One night, the mother lays down the last straw, saying abruptly: "If you ever want to get married, you'd better learn how to cook."

"But I do know how to cook!" replies Marianne, red as a rooster (and with no intention of marriage).

"Then why not make supper tomorrow?"

"Why not?"

"All right?"

"Okay."

All through the night that follows, Marianne tries to recall the easiest recipe she knows that isn't spaghetti or lasagne. She finally decides on her recipe for fish with croutons and cheddar cheese, one of the most reliable. The next day she sets off with a basket to do her shopping — unaware, though she has a faint suspicion, that she's heading for disaster.

She buys some fish, whatever white filets she sees — it's amazing how the names of fish vary from one language to another. It seems affordable but mysteriously, she's charged a steep price. Then she goes to buy cheese. Since nothing resembles extra-old Canadian cheddar, she discusses the recipe with the saleswoman.

"Fish and cheese, really?" asks the saleswoman, grimacing.

"Umm ... yes," replies Marianne, suddenly doubting her own existence.

"What kind of fish?"

"Well, umm, I don't know, a white fish. I haven't bought it yet," replies Marianne, hiding behind her back the bag whose smell clearly overwhelms that of the cheese.

"What kind of cheese do you want?" (Still unsmiling.)

"A kind that will melt in the oven."

"A hard cheese, then. Strong or mild?"

"Strong."

"All right then, this one?" pointing at the most expensive.

"Yes, all right, that one," Marianne resigns herself, seeing a substantial part of her fortune end up in a piece of cheese.

The saleswoman cuts the cheese, makes a greasy package of it, and leaning over the scale, she checks: "Cheese and fish, are you really sure?"

Next, Marianne goes to the bakery. The ideal bread for this recipe is the sliced, white, toaster-size milk bread that comes in a plastic bag. In the village there's no toaster and therefore no sliced bread. Marianne falls back on ordinary white bread, which tastes of nothing because it contains nothing. She tells herself that she could also turn it into French toast, just so Marco and his mother can finally taste the maple syrup she gave them as a present, which they stuck away on top of the highest cupboard between an Etruscan vase and a stuffed viper. She also buys parsley, an onion, and the makings of a salad that she'll serve with a real French vinaigrette.

She gets there around six. She realizes at once that the mother won't leave the kitchen and that she'll make it a point of honour to supervise operations, in particular to assure herself that she won't set fire to the house with the gas stove. Fine, thinks Marianne, who is capable of pride for a few hours more, at least I'll be able to show her how quickly I can slice vegetables.

The vegetables are lined up on the carving board and held there firmly with her left hand while the right one moves the knife from top to bottom, rapidly, its tip always in contact with the board. Her way of cutting vegetables seems to impress Marco's mother, who has stopped all activity to look on. But Marianne, aware of her eyes, cuts her index finger and gets onion juice in the cut.

The mother leaves the kitchen briefly and comes back with a Band-Aid. While Marianne chops the rest of the vegetables, she starts to unwrap the fish.

"So, you bought fish. What kind is it?"

Marianne, who of course doesn't know, counts on the fact that the mother will see the filet any second now.

"So, it's sole," says the mother. "Where did you get it?"

Suddenly Marianne remembers that she's in a family of fishermen and that Marco's cousin, the grandfather's worthy descendant, has a virtual monopoly on the sale of fish in the area. She has seen the huge house that he built at the top of a hill, she's seen his fish-farming tanks. In this terribly poor region, their name appears prominently, surrounded by a big red hook, on the front of all the village fish merchants and that of the factory where the fish is filleted before being shipped. The mother, herself a seasoned fish-filletter, works for the cousin occasionally. She makes it clear that her nephew always requests her help with extreme politeness and that she does him a favour by going to the plant. She's long past the age at which people generally retire. But even so, she hops on her old bicycle with the soft tires. When people see her in the stupefying sunlight on the main road, in a wool jacket and with a scarf around her neck, they realize at once that she'll be spending the day with the fish and the other filletters in the plant refrigerator. She works quickly with her hands and draws a minimal salary, how much no one knows but the bosses, who are careful to keep it to themselves. Glad to be working, proud to be working well, and mindful that she's contributing to the family business, the mother never asks herself any questions. She comes home just before supper. Through some strange phenomenon that may result from being exposed to fishing for all those years, she never brings home a fish smell. Sometimes, but rarely, she'll say that she's a little tired.

"Where did you get this fish?"

"On the Piazza della Fontana."

"And how much did the bastard make you pay?"

"Umm, well, it doesn't matter."

"A lot?"

"Not that much …"

"How much?"

Marianne tries to come up with an answer evasive enough to save her honour and precise enough to satisfy the other woman, who is rummaging in the package for the bill. She finds it.

"Could have been worse. Who sold it to you?"

"A man."

"How old?"

"White hair, balding, blue eyes."

"Glasses?"

"Right."

"Do you know who he is?"

"No."

The mother sticks out her chest as if she were about to disclose the fact that she holds the reins of western economy.

"My brother. With that accent of yours he could see that you're a foreigner and he figured, might as well take advantage of her, but next time you go there — now you listen to me — next time you say: 'Do you know who this fish is for?' He'll say: 'No, who?' And you'll say: 'For la Rosina,' that's what he calls me, 'it's for la Rosina and I want the best.'"

"All right," says Marianne, who's becoming irritable, and while becoming irritable, cuts into the Band-Aid with her knife and feels the onion juice in her cut again.

The mother gives her a quick and worried look, then goes back to rummaging in the grocery bags.

"Bread, parsley, garlic, I've got all that, you should have asked me. Mustard, of all things! We never eat that, you can take it to the other house. Shall I light the oven now? And if something's missing, let me know. Is there anything you need?"

My mother, thinks Marianne, Mamma, help, but she replies: "A big frying pan. Have you got any butter?"

"Yes. But oil would be better."

"No, butter."

"If you say so. Here's the butter."

Marianne browns her onion in the butter, she mustn't have adjusted the flame properly, the butter scorches, the onions burn. She adds parsley, bread, mustard (like it or not, the recipe calls for it). When it's time to add the cheese, she realizes that she's forgotten to grate it. She turns down the flame, asks for the grater — which takes several minutes because she doesn't know how to say "grater" or "grate," so she has to mime what she wants. The mother, perplexed, finally shows her the parmesan grater, which has tiny holes. "Sorry, it's all we've got."

Marianne starts to cut thin slices of cheese with a knife. She eats a bit while she's at it (she's famished) and is terror-stricken: it's totally bland. She doesn't dare add more mustard to make up for the lack of taste. Her throat tightens as she watches the cheese melt in the pan with the other ingredients that, while she was miming a grater, have turned pitifully limp. As it melts, the cheese forms fat lumps. Bravely, she spreads the shapeless mush over the raw fish filets and puts the result in the oven.

"Cheese with fish? Really?" asks the mother.

Marianne makes no reply. She starts to prepare the vinaigrette and the salad.

"Now that's a good idea, putting all the vegetables together. Watch out for your fingers."

"Yes."

"What are you doing?"

"Making the vinaigrette."

"Marco hates vinegar, you know."

"Yes, but with the other ingredients it doesn't taste so strong."

"Very well, do as you like, we'll see what he has to say. Wait and see before you put your vinaigrette on the salad."

"I'm making more, the full recipe, that way you'll have some in reserve."

"That's nice of you but no, I don't think so, take it all to the other house — your vinegar, your mustard, really, it's nice of you, but I don't think so, no."

Everything is ready. The fish, the salad, the vinaigrette. Marco doesn't appear. For a long time Marco doesn't appear. While Marco isn't appearing, the fish goes on slowly baking at the lowest temperature. At last he appears. He comes into the house, then leaves immediately to feed the dogs. He comes back, asks if he has time for a shower before supper, his mother says yes, Marianne says no. He washes his hands and sits down at the table.

Marianne takes the fish out of the oven. While she's arranging it on the plates, she sees it break apart. Overcooked. Very overcooked.

"What kind of fish is this?" asks Marco.

Marianne, who's forgotten the name of the fish again, is silent.

"Sole," says the mother.

"Where did you get it?"

"On the Piazza della Fontana."

"And how much did you pay?"

"Umm, well."

"A lot?"

"A little. It doesn't matter."

"Look, next time you buy something, now listen, I'll go with you. They'll understand who you are and then you won't have any problems."

"Okay. *Buon appetito.*"

They start eating the fish. The first mouthful confirms it: totally tasteless. As a result, Marianne has no appetite. "It's very good," says Marco's mother, standing up to get the salt. Marco says nothing. He shovels it in. He takes a second helping — he walked a lot that day.

"Look at the lovely salad," says the mother.

Marianne gets the vinaigrette and starts pouring it onto the salad.

"Hang on," says Marco, stopping her. "Is there vinegar in that?"

"Yes."

"Give me some salad without it. Have we got oil, Mamma? I like it with just oil."

Marianne can feel the mother looking at her. She expects her to smile, victorious, but when Marianne looks up, she sees her sympathizing. "All right," she thinks, "don't panic. I'll make up for it with the French toast, that's something I can make even before I've had coffee." She gets up, cuts the bread, soaks it in the mixture of egg, sugar, vanilla, and milk, and puts it into the frying pan where the butter is already melting.

So far, all is well: the fire is low, the butter doesn't burn. And then, suddenly, everything keels over again when she bends over the pan and, helpless, sees a skin form on the milk and the bread slowly dissolve, turning from a slice into a granular liquid inside the hard crust, which is derisively intact. "What a feast! Dry fish mush with tasteless cheese, another mush of bread and boiled milk. A dazzling revelation of my many talents."

Reduced to mush herself, she brings her guests huge plates of French toast (whose French name, lost bread, has never been more fitting) onto which, as compensation, she pours half the contents of the jug of maple syrup. The room temperature that evening is thirty-seven and when Marco and his mother tuck into their dessert, they begin to sweat copiously and their faces start to look like wax. They slow down more and more until they decide to push away their plates, Marco first and then his mother.

"Thank you, Marianne," they say, "it's not that it's bad, but here, you know, we aren't used to sweet desserts."

"It doesn't matter," says Marianne, getting up to clear the table, while Marco and his mother, slumped on their chairs, rub their stomachs.

When she sits down again the verdict falls, irrevocable. "Thanks," says the mother, "it was nice of you to make supper and we really did eat a lot."

And that's all. The mother will sleep well tonight, in spite of her digestive difficulties and her miasma of compassion, because in Marianne's mush she has seen the future, which she already knew: Marco will never leave.

When your mother dies you'll be alone with your dogs.

You'll be alone among the dogs, and you'll wish more than usual that you were a dog yourself. You'll eat pasta every day, and tomatoes with oil. Neither the pasta nor the tomatoes will taste like before, because you won't take the time to salt them properly or to put in the basil. Dead birds will pile up in your freezer, now and then you'll give one to friends, you'll also use them as bargaining chips. You'll stop shaking off your boots when you come in and you'll let the dogs sleep inside. You'll sweep up once a month, quickly, and limiting yourself to under the kitchen table. You'll never go to the cemetery. On your mother's grave — she who all her life put flowers on the graves of others — there will be none.

You'll hardly shed a tear, resolute forever in your isolation though it will weigh on you in a new way. You'll think about her every day. You'll sleep in her bedroom, which is bigger, but you won't change anything in it. You'll leave her clothes in the closet, her crochet work and yarn on a chair.

Your aunts will try to look after you, but you'll turn them down, politely. In spite of everything, you're very polite. Your politeness comes close to rudeness, it's so cold and automatic, it just shows how far removed from anyone else you want to be.

You'll miss certain things, a few little things such as never having learned to speak words of love, such as never having had the courage to leave home, and you'll know that your mother took with her to the grave, along with her recipe for stuffed turtledove, the recipes for love and courage. You'll know that it was from her that you'd have had to learn the proper words, and from her heart that you'd have had to snatch permission to leave. It will be too late and it will be no more important than today, because already you've given up, because you've welded your renunciation to your silence, because already you find in it the relative comfort to be found in any form of asceticism.

On the day of your mother's death you will go on living the way you did before, perhaps greeting a little more solemnly life's dark *intentions which you, an utter fatalist, have always greeted as they arrive, without trying to change anything at all.*

I'll be elsewhere then, and you'll have long since withdrawn from me the power to caress the thoughts that are in your head — all of which I loved without ever knowing them.

IV

EVERY DAY

*I*t's a field of dried sunflowers, their black faces bent towards the ground. Marco has on his blue work overalls with the straps tied at the small of his back, he is walking ahead of Marianne. She catches up with him, grabs hold of a strap, from the colour of her eyes he understands what she wants.

They retrace their steps. He carries her over his shoulders through the thorny bushes. They climb onto the boat that's hidden in the grass and in the slow sound of the lake and the early evening, between the reeds and close to another abandoned boat that's full of water, in no time their knees are full of splinters, Marco's fabulous eyes are shot through with the fleeting sun, his back set with pebbles, water falls from his forehead drop by drop onto Marianne's throat, his eyes are closed, then open, then closed again and in a little while, when they're back on terra firma, their legs will still be trembling between the sunflowers.

It's nothing, it's so little. It takes so little in the beginning to make Marianne happy. The first sentence spoken in the newly acquired language without one mistake; the thick, phosphorescent green of the olive oil; a magnificent rainfall that clears the beach and transforms the surface of the water into a carpet of metallic grasshoppers; the vigorous way the dogs run through the fields, and the mist that escapes from their muzzles; the splayed red interior of ripe figs; the immensity of the lake beneath her avid strokes; their gravelly accent when they pronounce her name; the handful of basil the salesman puts in with the tomatoes, its piquant taste rubbing off on the peaches in the same bag. The lining of joy is bitter from the outset however, because Marianne soon realizes that it has no resonance here at all outside herself, that joy, this particular joy, her own, cannot be communicated.

At the table around two p.m. Marco's remark, always the same, drops like a blade: "Okay, I'm off now, do whatever you want." So she won't hear it, Marianne often rushes out as soon as she's cleaned her plate. You never know exactly where Marco is on his way to. He says "to work," but that's actually a generic term. Marianne sees him from a long way off, chatting with other men on the terrace of a bar, and his sailboards are always on the roof of his Jeep. Actually, he works as little as possible, just enough to earn what he needs for the mortgage payments; he leaves plumbing in the lurch and his customers without water as soon as he can afford to. She both admires and scorns the way he fills his days with trivial chitchat and little lies, the way he goes through life with no urgency, filling it with whatever he fancies.

Now and then he parks outside the empty house. Because of the stone wall, Marianne can't see the car, but she recognizes out of all others the sound of the engine that's become her obsession. He takes her for an iced tea or to feed the ducks. As she never knows if Marco will come by, she keeps her ear pricked. And on the street, she can't help glancing furtively over her shoulder. He shows up sometimes, like a mushroom suddenly emerging from the ground. She sticks messages on the door for him: I'm at the lake, I'm at the hotel, I'm in the village drawing, I've gone for a walk in the harbour. At first she's reluctant to do it because, she thinks, the neighbours will also know where she's gone. But remembering that everyone always knows everything in any case, she sticks her messages on the door. She has come to live with him. She doesn't let him lose track of her, because she knows that he could. Because he does lose track, obstinately. Never does he take advantage of the little notes, all of which she'll keep in memory of God knows what.

She accepts his absence, though it makes her suffer, because that absence is him. It's his way of owning himself: free. She knows that he expects from her a similar freedom, and during the first weeks she takes every measure to be fully occupied by her own affairs. Until she understands what she hadn't understood before: her need of a world. To exercise her freedom, she needs a world. She needs a world in which freedom is used to overcome the inertia of the world and to flow with its movement. She also understands that the world does not start out as a landscape or a work or an administrative procedure undertaken with a view to obtaining a residence permit, the world doesn't even consist of the need to drink or eat: she understands that the world is other people. That is well expressed in fact in the French saying: "It takes a lot of people to make a world." In that language, a single word, *monde*, means both people and the place where they're located, and it's because a place is its people. In Marco's country, Marianne has no world. She speaks to individuals who don't reply, who are content to accumulate information about her that they can pass on to a cousin or an aunt, that for two or three minutes will give them the upper hand. In this absurd situation, Marco himself becomes the entire world, though he is unquestionably the individual least qualified and least willing to become someone else's world.

A letter arrives now and then to remind her that she too exists elsewhere, with the density of a normal individual. But a letter is a very modest testimony. It is the residue of a moment in the life of a friend two weeks ago. A few times the phone rings for her. She picks it up, awkwardly, surprised by the simultaneity of her voice and the one over there. She can never articulate anything at all and that difficulty says a lot about the distance she's thrown into, the opacity of the mist that she fades into while she waits for Marco, who doesn't come, and while she works relentlessly to at least stay contemporary with herself, detached from all continents of reality but still secured to a shred of herself, to the memory of her self that is hard to grasp, lost as it is like one drop among raindrops.

A fisherman makes fast his boat to a metal ring. He stops for a moment and observes Marianne.

"What are you doing?"

"I'm drawing."

"What are you drawing?"

"The boats."

"Where's mine?"

"It will be here."

"Are you a foreigner?"

"Yes."

"German?"

"No."

"What then?"

"Canadian."

"What did you say?"

"I come from Canada."

"Ah. How long will you be staying?"

"I don't know."

"Are you staying at the hotel?"

"No."

"Where then?"

Marianne gestures vaguely in the direction of her street.

"What number?"

"Three."

"Ah!"

The man's face lights up.

"You're Marco's girlfriend."

"That's right."

He stares at her for a moment, pensive.

"Good old Marco."

Suddenly Marianne notices the striking resemblance between the fisherman and Marco's mother. As she knows that chances are she won't be mistaken, she asks: "Are you his uncle?"

He's stupefied.

"That's right. I'm his uncle. You're staying in the house where I grew up."

"Ah!"

"I'm not too interested in what happens on the ground. I caught an eel today. Some day maybe you could draw an eel, they're very pretty."

The evening meal, when Marco is there, unfolds like lunch. Fulli meets her on the doorstep. He leads the way into the kitchen, turning around two or three times during the very brief walk to make sure she's following, visibly eager to be a good host.

Fulli is the only one who comes to welcome her. Approaching her, he also tries to overcome his jealousy, his painful awareness that he's just the eldest of the dogs and that unlike her, he doesn't have the privilege of climbing onto the bed. During the meal, he lies on the floor, as close to the table as possible, and sometimes, without realizing it, he steps on the mother's foot and she shoves him aside, cursing. When Marianne has finished eating, he checks out of the corner of his eye (hidden by fur) that she has stopped using her fork, then he comes and lays his head on her lap. Every time, Marco says, "Fufu, no, leave her alone," but in this very precise situation, Fulli waits for Marianne to say the final word. Sometimes she says no and Fulli, head down and tail dragging, turns around and stretches out on the floor. Generally though she says nothing, she pets him and he lets his head weigh more and more heavily on her lap; he slobbers abundantly and keeps an eye on her. Marianne is well aware that he's the only one, that he'll always be the only one, to approach her without demanding that she reinvent herself, without demanding anything but her right hand on his big hairy head.

After a while Marianne gets up and goes out. Marco — if he doesn't fall asleep at the table — will join her in an hour or two. In the empty house she doesn't turn on any lights. If it's windy, she opens the windows. If he comes, Marco always says: "You're in the dark." Always, she replies: "Yes, I'm in the dark," and as the evenings pass she thinks that her reply is more and more pertinent. Marco switches on lights along the way. Invariably, he asks: "What do you want to do?" though they both know there's absolutely nothing to do, except maybe have a beer at the bar or walk the dogs just outside the national park. They'll go for a beer, then they'll walk the dogs.

In the morning, at five o'clock, Marco gets up, gets dressed, and leaves.

Every day is a desert.

And yet, in the nighttime forest, two stone basins collect water from a hot spring. They take off their clothes. Night is opaque on their skins, the stone slippery under their feet, slowly Marco immerses himself in one of the basins. He crouches, sighs with contentment, lets the small amount of water cover his shoulders; he holds out his arms, in the shadow you can see his white smile floating like a firefly. Marianne puts her feet in the basin and plunges her body into the tangled arms of the warm water and the man.

She is madly in love with this body. Stocky, tanned, lithe, perfectly adapted to each of his movements, as if all of them, no matter what they are, originated in an absolute necessity and took their form from an ancient design: walk energetically, almost vertically, open the hand the precise amount required by the object to be grasped, let it describe the discourse in space, smile abruptly, a smile that holds a pleasure forever new. This body that smells of green leaves and dead leaves, that moves among other bodies: she loves the way clothes fit on it and conceal it, she loves the privilege of its nakedness. When this body is cold, when it trembles, how perfectly it resists the wind; the moment when this body topples into ecstasy and then into sleep, the imperceptible change in his breathing, becoming deep, irregular, and his way of waking with a start at the slightest sound of footsteps. She loves this body, madly, that madness will be her downfall, she knows that, but still it contains the kernel of desire, the animal truth of living heat. She goes towards this body, it's an irresistible and disastrous progression that she consents to with all her strength and that her newly regained strength greets as a miracle.

He holds her against him. For a long time they stay that way, naked and together, unmoving. Above them, the darkness has hair of lightning, one tower of the castle offers its crenellations between obstinate pines, the night is vast, they are two, one, barely. A mass coiled in the stone basin, swallowed by the woods. Each of them given back to the first darkness, they say nothing — there is nothing to say.

"Would you donate your body to science?" Marianne asks Marco.

They're driving in the mountains. Marco knows all the dirt roads, he prefers them to the paved ones, he often drives on them for the simple pleasure of emerging into a field, of loudly losing his temper with a wildcat that's lying in wait for the same prey he is, or of seeing a pheasant panic at the dogs' barks, forget he has wings, and run across the road with urgent, frenzied little steps.

"No. You?"

"Sure. Why not?"

"Because it's mine."

"But if you die it's of no use."

"It's still mine though, isn't it? Just as your body belongs to you, doesn't it?"

"I've always thought it was a kind of loan."

"Who are you then?"

"Me."

"And who's you?"

"Me."

"The rest, outside your body?"

"Maybe."

"No, listen, you aren't being clear — you rarely are, by the way — what else is there?"

"The soul maybe?"

"What's that? You always use that word, what does it mean?"

"I don't know any more than you do."

"*Ma dai*, if you use the word you must know what it means, right?"

"It's the kernel."

"Of a peach or a grape?"

"Same thing."

"I prefer the flesh."

"The flesh comes from the kernel."

"That's true. So you believe in the eternity of the soul."

"Probably. You?"

"No."

"And when a person dies?"

"What do I know about that?"

"But you talk to your father now and then, you told me."

"Maybe I'm talking to myself."

"But the meaning of life — don't you every wonder about it?"

"No."

"I'll ask you then: what is the meaning of life?"

"It's ... to live."

"And that's it?"

"Yes. I'm at home here."

"Here?"

"In life."

"In your body?"

"In my body, which is in life."

"But that, your body, doesn't it ever seem foreign to you?"

"Sometimes I'm in pain or tired, but it's *my* pain and *my* fatigue."

"You never feel the need to get closer?"

"To what?"

"To the world."

"No. You?"

"It's hard for me to have fallen into the world."

"You've fallen into the world?"

"Or the world fell on me, who knows?"

"And before it fell, where were you?"

"I was complete."

"But I don't lack anything here, I eat, I sleep, I drink, you're there, look at those trees, they produce fruit for us, they have seeds for the next trees, and when the hunting season opens there'll be ducks — but maybe not in November, hunters are idiots you know, they kill everything they see at the very beginning of the season. Look, Marianne, the sun's out, what don't you have?"

"The world."

"Still, it's there, the world is there."

"But it always seems that it's not for me."

"No, no, that's not true, it's there, it's there to be taken. Not to steal, mind you — you know, some hunters are stupid, they kill more animals than they can eat — it's there when we need it, it's there for us because we're part of the world."

"You're right."

"No, no, it's just the way I think, that's all."

"For you living is quite natural."

"Well sure, it's totally natural."

"And death?"

"What?"

"Are you afraid of dying?"

"No, but I'd like to live as long as possible. I'm at home on the earth. I'd like to be immortal. Tell me what you don't have that you need."

"To be able to fly."

"To fly? There's the sky, it's made for that. There's the big bed in the little house, it's made for that, Marianne, it's made for flying."

"In Quebec it's cold for six months of the year."

"And what about your soul, do you warm it every day?"

"That's what I'm trying to tell you."

"Come and live with me then."

"That's what I'm trying to do."

"Come on, we'll both be immortal."

Later, Marco stops the car to pick a giant artichoke blossom, mauve and white, its leaves pointing towards every corner of the earth at once.

They enter into one another, it's their most natural state, the most reassuring, the closest to the state in which one is fully part of the world. Impetuous in the cold tender in the heat in the rain in the morning in the fields slowly at night scarcely stormy again lost new eternal until — eternal. As if their bodies were naturally one single body eager to recognize itself. Desperately searching for its own code. As if it were foreseen. As if what was foreseen were to be embodied, urgently, before the separation that had itself been foreseen and feared, because already that had happened too. As if it were a question of being not yet born, knowing that it wouldn't be long: the breaking of the waters. Groping, they try to find a form for God, in the other's moans they hear the suffering of his personification and his wild animal's sensual ecstasy. It's a tremendous job. It is their way of speaking the same language, each knowing they're understood and confirmed, beyond any possible doubt, in their similar hearts. These hours snatched from reality give them the certainty that they have everything to live for, each in the other, the one for the ecstasy of the other, and that is why there is between them no coyness, no hesitation, there is the disproportionate power of placing one's hand there, where desire can be sensed, there, where it will presently, immediately drift into pleasure — the mere beginning of a caress is enough sometimes, or a way of stretching one's neck, of unlacing a shoe, sometimes it takes them the whole night to arrive, exhausted, trembling with the knowledge of the other, overwhelmed by their way of letting go.

I write every morning so as to keep at hand the words "sun" and "flower" — I am poor. I do it to imagine that my pencil moving across the page perforates the paper straight to the dogs' barking, and there are times when I'm able to be nothing more than this place, with no stopping or fatigue, and in spite of everything.

Small gestures are what keep us alive, yet their smallness creates the urge to die. Through the sound of plates in the sink, between my toes and the cotton sheet; with your absence hidden like a frog beneath the warmth of everyday things, it might have been better to hope for nothing. I wish my belongings could fit into one cardboard box, light, then I could leave again, to anywhere at all.

At the airport, when the customs officers have gone through my suitcase and confiscated the sunflowers I'd brought back, they also studied, perplexed, the artichoke blossom, the distraught expression on my face and the dried face of the flower, and they gave it back to me a moment later so I could put it in my room next winter, which was going to be long, very long, just by looking at my face they knew, it was an omen better than onion skins: the next winter was going to be a hard one.

The knot on your overalls is as remote from me as a Chinese film, as a nineteenth-century novel, as a half-repressed dream. As remote as patent leather shoes for pre-kindergarten; as the branches swept along the St. Lawrence to Sorel or Baie-Saint-Paul, to the sea; as the chalet where I spent whole summers pulling my brother's hair. On the village square, between the clock and the men's bar where you've never let me buy you a coffee, under a rain of scales played by mediocre students, stands the strong part of my soul, my faith. It can still perhaps be heard knocking at your door, and on very windy nights, spreading its arms open on the harbour promenade, hoping for a storm that would break before long — my faith.

I placed in my bedroom the giant artichoke blossom you picked at the end of a difficult road, and in its spines I see all of you. My emptiness is this: having had to cut myself away from my faith and to live now on the remains of the day, knowing vaguely that I was right to leave, not finding in any face here the luminous trace of yours; yet searching for it relentlessly, straining in a search as slippery as a bar of soap, struggling to engage myself in what surrounds me only to discover that I'm no longer engaged. My faith: it drinks a wine whose cork explodes into a blossom of gaiety and it smiles the way all of you smile, free of ambition. There, in the main square, my faith is hot at four p.m. and cold around midnight, I see it waiting for me, whispering: don't come back, I can't be here, look for me somewhere else, I won't move.

It won't move from your village until I've found the other place where I can grasp it again. It is lodged in a metaphysical space and if I were so extravagant as to take the plane, the train, and the bus that would drop me off at the foot of the clock some week-night at five after six, I wouldn't be able to recognize it. It is waiting for me there, where I'll be strong enough to travel again. It stays with you, who are no longer a journey but only the residue of the most wonderful of journeys. It stays there, waiting for me to find the other window through which I'll fly away, waiting until I take a step in the life of my life whatever it might be — my faith: in the meantime I must bear its looking at me from so far, from so high, and lacking the wings to reach it.

I would like your memory to be the counterpart of mine. You, who have known only the extreme fringes where you took me without noticing, who invented for me, invisibly, the continent fit to live in, the undying continent, the happy excess — I am here now, in my country the winter is long, it's hard, and I have so much to do to reinvent myself.

"You don't say anything about yourself."

"There's nothing to say."

"Why did you become a plumber?"

"So I could work on my own."

"And you like your work?"

"A person has to earn a living."

"What do you like most when we're in bed?"

"Everything."

"Why do you always use the vulgar word for 'making love'?"

"Because 'making love' is a lot wider."

"Meaning?"

"'To make love' means everything that's done for love, right?"

"For instance?"

"For instance, to talk."

"I see."

"Like that it's more precise."

"Do you think that Fulli and Argo talk to you?"

"No. Yes. With their tails. And Fulli can smile, have you noticed?"

"No."

"Look at the moon. How many days till it's full?"

"Twenty-eight."

"It's easy to see you're from the city."

"What?"

"Take a good look."

"Oh. Fourteen."

"You should look at it more often."

"Do you talk with your mother?"

"Never."

"What does she know about me?"

"Nothing."

"Do you think she hopes that I'll leave?"

"Why?"

"To be sure that you won't go away."

"That's my business."

"Will you come to my country?"

"Maybe."

"No, never."

"Yes, maybe never."

I loved you in your silence, the silence of a man rebelling against the mystery of women, and I waited for you every day, the way I used to wait for my father at supper time, at the foot of an old oak tree. My father taught me about everyday absence and about presence restored, he also taught me the meaning of a promise, the meaning of the other, who is implacably other, who encourages us to become ourselves through waiting, and being alone while we wait. You've always kept yourself outside me, which was fine, which was fine until I realized that you'd never come by and take me beside the oak tree, that you would let me wait for you and wear myself out from waiting. My father came without fail, he would sit me on his knees as we drove down the gravel road. Probably that's also the reason why I had to leave you.

Marco asks for nothing more than for what happens to him. He "works." Fall and winter, he hunts. On windy days, he goes wind surfing, on dull days, he talks about the weather with people he's never attached to. He has no friends, or very few, friends who know nothing about him because he never says anything. There are friends whom he's lost, a good many, friends he's broken with for various reasons, the main one being that he has no pity for the human race.

Marco is faithful to himself, he is faithful to his dogs. He eats at his mother's house twice a day, he deals with his bills and makes mortgage payments on time. He is faithful to his hunger, to his thirst, to his need for sleep, regardless of when, regardless of where. Even if he loved other women, Marco would be faithful in his way, faithful to his desire; and that fidelity, which she admires, enables Marianne to accept anything.

Marco is faithful to the life for which he was born. He complains about it for the sake of form but never changes it. His body is faithful to his life, just dark enough that he doesn't suffer in the sun, just muscular enough that he needs to make no effort. He's never gone to a dentist, his teeth are remarkable, and when he takes aim at a bird on the wing, he never misses.

Marco's silence is faithful to his way of speaking. There are times when he's silent and times when he speaks, and the difference between those two states, surprising though it may be for those around, means nothing to him.

When Marianne enters the perfect mechanism of Marco's life, she moves like a mouse so as not to break anything, though she understands that she is in the process of digging a hole which she'll leave gaping open on the day of her departure, understanding as well that she will never possess Marco's grandiose modesty, the quiet joy of days that are all the same, and along which time seems to move by accident. Numbers shouldn't matter. See you later or tomorrow.

His bedroom in his mother's house is cramped, with a camp cot, too soft; hunting trophies and sailboards; the material he needs for making cartridges; pheasant feathers and open doors; dog-eared books; cassettes; an Italian-English dictionary; an Italian-French dictionary.

His room is a mess, his garden and garage are a mess. Any neat areas are his mother's. Marco's untidiness is limited to where it's allowed. It is contained within itself, small packages left there, abandoned to the goodwill of space. His way of neglecting objects is very gentle. It's not forced or aggressive, it's not opposed to anything: it is quite simply the tremendous flexibility of reality at ease in its present state. It simply *is*, like the growth of weeds.

Above his bed floats his diving gear, like a limp body covered with dust. It is suspended from the cupboard where his mother methodically puts his clean clothes. Marianne is terrified of that hanged man. One night when she asks him how he can sleep with it there, he replies, shrugging: "What's to be scared of? It's just me."

Marco has never thought about suicide, is even surprised that such a thought exists. On the other hand, he is obsessed with the imminence of some deadly disaster, with a predilection for a viper's bite, though he acknowledges a mass of variations — another hunter's rifle; the drowning of those who eat too much melon; a surfer surprised by a storm; car accidents; bombings; bad falls; food poisoning.

One afternoon, he even asks Marianne to come to the garage with him. He wants to show her two long white boxes intended for storing fish. They're from his cousin and he'd like to use them for transporting his hunting gear.

He pauses, then says: "It's too bad, they're perfect — light and roomy, and they fit in the Jeep ..."

"But?"

"Whenever I see them I think about coffins and it sends a chill up my spine."

Surprised by this confession, Marianne takes a box and stands it in front of Marco, who is a good head taller.

"Look, it's too small for you."

"But with my legs cut off?"

"Yes, but anyway, if you're cut into pieces you'd fit into a garbage bag, too."

Marco doesn't reply, but in the garage the following week, Marianne notices that the boxes have gone. Death frightens him only insofar as it will come from outside, to break the equilibrium of his normal, enjoyable life. Because of this, paradoxically, Marco likes to say that he's immortal.

Immortal because within the limits of his enjoyable life, there's no set time for going to bed; because he can go without coffee one day and drink twelve cups the next; because he only shaves once a year, on no fixed date; because his car is falling apart; because he's poor and works so seldom. Marco says he's immortal: that's because he knows he is mortal, which suits him fine. On one side there is life and on the other, death. During life, we live. Death is simply the completion of that verb.

I've put a table in a huge room where the sun stays lazily all morning. I sit at it, I look outside, I look at a tree that's carving a place for itself in the icy sky, I watch the cold cracking the roof of the front neighbour's house.

Your arms had a strange way of embracing me, then letting me go right away, as if to avoid holding me, as if to avoid making promises: as if to refuse for themselves the help that everyone needs, help that you actually don't want to take from or give to anyone.

We only really topple over within ourselves. Why not call the essential presences, recognize them when they touch down like white butterflies on the edge of our eyelids, thank them for coming, welcome them home before nightfall, and become for them — and for others too — the light in the countryside at night that I'm crazy about, the light that's on at night, keeping watch on the balcony of the chalet, so that nearby insects in the thousands will come and keep watch too — one could become that, that quiet sifted space of almost nothing, and sleep then, deeply confident, at the side of one's waking and vigilant self.

I wish I could have loved you starting from life. I'd have had to lose you on the horizon, let you blend with things that are loved simply for their power of being. I'd have had to love you no more and no less than a tired footstep sinking into the beach, with that way the sand has of filling in the arch of the foot without losing anything of its own shape. From you I was trying to extract a first love, then expand it to everything and distribute it like the crumbs of stale bread that we throw to the birds. I should have loved you in reverse, loved you because you arrive in addition to what already is, because you are the bluer shade of the water and the brighter patch of sky, coolness added to the shadow of the leaves: like the abundance of the already-loved. I should have loved you as if I were finding a new way of greeting things. Loving should happen in the impossible patience of the being, untangling from you the brittle threads of expectation and disappointment, so you would never be deprived of yourself, and so I would not be so bereft once your image has disappeared.

I spread a cloth on the table, it's the colour of a salmon and there are flowers woven into it. Last night I dreamed that I was swimming in a lake full of water weeds. I wanted to cross the lake but none of the shores was the right one, I was tired, hungry, I woke up thirsty. On an island along the way I saw a church whose steps dropped abruptly into the water, it was old, dirty, its walls were full of holes, it had a flat, pink front, it was beautiful, I would have liked to go inside.

In my vast window I hung plants so that when I'm writing I won't see the terrifying breadth of the sky. That way the sky is not so high, but it is as deep as ever, infinitely deep. I write out of a profound fatigue. I'm stupid, I'm tense, I am sitting at the table set for happiness, the sun blazes onto my pencil, my index finger, my thumb, I don't write anything. I am a pink wall, dirty, flat, old, I'm an old wall full of holes.

My cycle is twenty-eight days, almost to the hour. My body makes its way in the dimness just as well as in the light, I am blind. I try not to smoke, I try to eat properly. It's not much, to tell the truth, under the pneumatic drill.

When you reread pages that you've written you're surprised at having lost the trace of your hesitations, of strikeouts, of all the time spent cleaning your nails, drinking coffee, staring at the white wall. Despairing of literature, despairing of solitude — and expecting everything from them as well. Wishing the phone would ring, even a wrong number. I have a slight headache. I think my head is short of storage space. If there were one more drawer I would lay you down in it, with your dogs, your mother, and the figs, I'd lay down there for good your country's eternal sun, then I'd close the drawer, close it and lock it.

Sometimes people cry on airplanes, no one talks to them, the flight attendants walk straight ahead with their trays of fruit salad and ham, others who see them cry wonder what they've left behind in the other country, the country that's already tiny down below, that's no more than a sock lying on the ocean floor, their immense sorrow no more than a stain riddled with clouds. Between Rome and

Montreal, in the plane where I sat crying, a man died. Over the P.A. system they asked if there was a doctor on board, like in a bad movie. They asked in French, in English, in Italian, and yes, there was a doctor on board, who even spoke the three languages. Because I'd made my reservation at the last minute, my seat was near the place where they store flight equipment and also, as I learned that day, corpses. They quickly closed the curtain but I saw the dead man's bare feet, young feet, and I was surprised that I wasn't there instead of him. "The idea, to die on a plane," one flight attendant whispered into another's ear. It was death that had had the idea, death's own ideas which are neither good nor bad, but just the last ones.

When I took the plane in the opposite direction, to your country, I'd thought that since I would be living somewhere else, I would finally feel as if I were everywhere at once, and as a result that I was where I was supposed to be. I had taken your village for the entire universe. As if one could travel the whole universe on foot in less than half an hour, slowly, try every gelato in every bar and, in less than two weeks, find the best one, on the avenue of via degli Alberi. No. I'm condemned to be merely the small amount of space in which to move my body, and above it the exasperating hope that the sky provides, by dint of being the same for us all.

And you. You are a perfect microcosm. About you, I made no mistake. You are a kind of universe, as are people who die on airplanes, those who make the best gelato in the village, and those who look ravaged like a willow. That's what I know at this moment, as the winter advances: the country where one is supposed to live doesn't appear on maps. The country where one is supposed to live is humanity.

And I see clearly how at certain blessed moments, the question of location loses all significance, because reality starts to speak our imaginary language. Before coming back to you, I exhibited my paintings to pay for the second plane ticket. For the show I wrote something about the search for places fit to live in. I listed openings that seem insignificant but are important in their way. One of them stood out for no reason, it was a weird metaphor, it had no resonance, it was foreign to my patience and I resisted it in vain. It was: "A blue marble found in a hole in the sand."

One afternoon, your cousin's wife decided to bring me along when she went fishing. She took a detour to the farm of a friend to whom she'd brought tins to fill with oil. The farm, a tall house on a vast estate, was dozing against an overexposed sky. An old man was snoring in a wicker chair, his eyes half-closed; a woman full of exclamations came towards us, smiling, asking for news, offering us coffee, and behind her voice unfurled the infinite ribbon of the hens' race before the little rooster's ciao bella, lengthened the pace of the wind in the olive trees. Everything was at once humble, calm, and bore no trace of waiting.

While the women jabbered, I played with the toes of my shoes in the sandy earth. I touched a round, shiny object and bent down to free it from the ground. It was so simple and insignificant: I'd just found a blue marble in a hole in the sand. The metaphor had got ahead of reality, it was a defective chronology thanks to which another metaphor became accessible, the marble suddenly saying in its inverted language: Yes, don't worry, you're exactly where we've been waiting for you; don't worry about anything, just notice how objects are speaking a familiar language.

The grandfather was smiling at me. I held the marble out to him, he gestured for me to keep it. I don't know where it is now, I put it in my pocket, it must have fallen out. Maybe it's waiting in some other hole in some other sand, waiting for someone to find it, for someone, finding it, to recognize it, and in recognizing it, feel at last that he is part of a legible world.

V

SWEAT

Da Nerone, Ristorante: six kinds of grappa, lager, dark ale, stout, exotic pizzas, wallet-emptying *secondi*, desserts accompanied by *Prosecco*; a former mill accessible by an ivy-covered staircase; the night lit by candles, placemats decorated attractively with animals, thick, bluish glasses, reflections perched on the mirrors and the brass trays, casks of beer, chrome and porcelain.

The owner, Grazia, has buckteeth, a skeletal face, coal-black hair pulled into a very long braid. She throws herself at Marianne whenever she sees her, like a sparrow hawk on a sleeping prey. Marianne has been warned about her, but Grazia uses a seductive tone to entice her: "Come and join us." "Here, for you, we're always open." "I'm expecting you, don't forget me." In short, she has a knack for stating the words of welcome that Marianne expects — in vain — from the village in general and from Marco in particular. The work Grazia offers seems in any case the only possible kind in a region plagued by unemployment, where hope lasts only as long as a tourist season.

And so, one day, Marianne goes there, as much from courage as from resignation. Grazia gives her a half-smile, takes her into the kitchen, explains that she'll work first at the bar, then at the tables. "The tables?" exclaims Mario, her husband, who's just made his entrance, "but she hardly knows a word of Italian, it would be a disaster!" "Don't worry," replies Grazia, who always has the last word, "she speaks enough to be understood and little enough to be charming." Marianne's throat tightens, she smiles idiotically, waits.

In July and August, the temperature is usually around thirty-five. Mario and Grazia have asked Marianne to wear black pants and she comes to work three times a week in new jeans that stick to her legs and are covered with beer, lemonade, and pizza sauce. Her shift starts at five o'clock. Mario puts on some music, the staff prepare the dining rooms. The wooden tables and the benches have to be lined up on the uneven flagstones of the terrace. Every night, Grazia scolds Mario, pointing out how wobbly they all are. "You have to do something, we can't let people eat there." Every night, without a word, Mario deals with the problem using cardboard coasters — three under one leg, two under the other — and the operation carries on with quality controls that always end with deep sighs. Employees set the tables with hundreds of knives, forks, spoons. Ashtrays, candlesticks, glasses. Then sit down for their own meal. Just as they're swallowing the first bite, Grazia leaps out of her seat and signals, shouting, that it's time to get down to work.

Foreigners eat early. They turn up around seven, ask Marianne to translate the menu, consider everything *sehr schön*, and tuck in, smiling. The Italians all arrive at the same time, around nine o'clock, driving up the blood pressure of the waitresses, the bartender, the cook, the *pizzaiolo*, and Grazia. Mario, between two flying trays, serves himself the first beer, dark, his favourite. As he brings it slowly to his mouth, the others are running every which way, bringing bread, salt, oil, wine, taking an order, frothing a beer that's stood around too long, washing a glass, foaming milk for a cappuccino, and answering the bell that from the second floor announces the birth of a pizza. A customer becomes impatient because his dish hasn't arrived, another wants to know all about winter in Quebec, and it's impossible to fathom the order of a couple sitting right under the speakers.

There's enough work for ten, there are only six, counting the dishwasher.

Sometimes fuses blow and darkness falls over the restaurant like a blessing. In the kitchen, the only thing that can be seen is the gas flames, and they all think, "Thank God." "Thank God," someone murmurs. But Grazia, spouting blasphemy, attacks the generator and, in under two minutes, has got the power back on, snatched the *crostini* from the oven, mechanically garnished three plates with cherry tomatoes and black olives, and placed them on Marianne's right hand — her left already holds a giant pizza. Mario, wanting to pour himself a second beer in the dark, has selected the wrong cask, and regretfully offers the glass of lager to the closest customer — on the house.

Every time she goes into the kitchen, it seems to Marianne that she sees exactly the same scene: the cook's bent back and her aching legs, the encouragement lavished by the dishwasher, Grazia's brusque gestures, where you can see in fits and starts, as in a futurist painting, the passage of tomatoes and olives onto elegant plates, sprinkled with slander yet digested serenely by the clientele.

Around a quarter to midnight, the restaurant is the only place in town that's still open — aside from the fruit store run by a depressive and tremulous old man who'd prefer not to see anyone though he can't bring himself to retire. It's suddenly peaceful — peaceful enough that the employees have time to identify faces and to keep in mind the geography of the tables. With one hand, Mario smoothes his hair, frizzy from the heat, and smiles miserably whenever he meets Marianne. He sighs, his lips quiver, his eyes are wet, he sips his beer, and declares: "One day, soon, I'll leave all this and get myself a guitar." Marianne picks up a tray, clears a table, comes back with an order for the bartender. "Yes, I'm going to leave," Mario repeats, tragically. "When?" she asks. "Soon," he answers, "soon." His wife emerges from the kitchen, slamming the door with her iron hand, looks at them for a moment, then shoves three plates into Marianne's hand and sends her with them to a table that wasn't assigned to her. She pushes Mario behind the cash register, tells him to calculate the bills, and when Marianne comes back, shoves them at her. "Soon, really?" Looking down, he finishes his beer in one gulp. "*Dai!*" says Grazia impatiently.

Every night Marianne has a moment to watch the moon resting on the roof across the way. On her empty tray, a summer insect sometimes touches down, or a white moth or, towards the end of the season, a dead leaf falling off the ivy. The restaurant overlooks the sleeping village, black against the black of the sky, you can hardly make out the shadow of a chapel tower and that of the combined angles of all the roofs together. I am here, thinks Marianne, here in the gorgeous night of this generous country. This night resembles mine, it's the same temperature as my skin and its warm passage goes along with all the rest, with those who are asleep and those who are awake and those who will soon go fishing. In this blonde countryside, from which all day she is excluded, she is surprised to discover the tremendous fidelity of the night, its discreet bandage on the scales of evil, the sublime refuge it offers from the scorching heat, the opening of its arms — black, blue, white. Night deposits on the tray its dust of darkness and moonlight, weightless and utterly soothing. A howl from Grazia pulls her from her meditation: a customer has spilled his beer and Mario is hurtling down the cellar stairs.

And then, at midnight, everything is ruined again. The restaurant is transformed into a bar and a new clientele, young and in many cases already drunk, shows up all at once, like a busload of Japanese at the Vatican. Everything's sailing on beer and the rumbling of voices, full glasses drop onto the floor tiles, couples make out in the shelter of candlelight. Every night, the customers at one table, never the same ones, realize that Marianne doesn't understand their dialect and they make risqué jokes while she waits for their orders, ill at ease, pencil suspended, and circles under her eyes. The staff's fatigue progresses beyond hunger, and now they're only energized by exasperated murmurs that drive them mechanically from table to table and from the bar to the pizzeria.

Finally, around a quarter past two, the pizzeria shuts down. At that exact moment, and as if acting with remarkable clair-voyance, a client orders a *focaccia* with rosemary, provoking the same discussion every night. Marianne to Mario: "Can we still serve a pizza?"

"No, the pizzeria's closed."

Then, seized with one last scruple, Mario to Grazia: "The pizzeria's closed, right?"

"No, no, one more, it's barely a quarter past two."

"But the *pizzaiolo* turned off the oven."

"Then he can turn it back on for God's sake, it's a sale, after all."

"But ..."

"*Dai!*"

Mario to Marianne: an apologetic look. Marianne to the *pizzaiolo*: sick at heart. The *pizzaiolo*: a sigh and grin from cheek to flour-covered cheek. He turns on the oven.

Shortly before three, the last customers leave or are discreetly thrown out by Mario when Grazia's back is turned. He starts early on nights when Paolo (father dead, brought up by his mother, a concierge on the outskirts of Rome, abandoned by his fiancée two days before their marriage, and famous throughout the region for surviving a suicidal leap from a moving train) comes in for a beer, then another. He may not have fallen under the train, but on those nights he collapses under the table, risks being swept up with the dust and the butts by employees anxious for bed. Mario, feeling no pain himself, bends over him and shakes him by the shoulders. Before Paolo's head hits the table, Mario tells him he'll soon be getting a guitar and going away, then grabs his feet, drags him to the stairs, and splashes his face with the water for the plants and with genuine compassion.

The staff upend the chairs on the tables, wash the floor with water full of ammonia, brush the stairs with water full of ammonia, scrub down the kitchen with water full of ammonia. Mario turns off the music to count the money in the cash and on good nights, he'll sing. He pours himself one last beer, offers one to Marianne — "Take your medicine" — and sometimes gives in as well to the pleas of the bartender, who isn't old enough yet. Between three and five every morning, the place is cleaned from top to bottom and a tireless Grazia runs from one employee to another, lavishing advice: "Put more water in your bucket, drag it along the floor if you can't lift it, come on, hurry up, I've got other things to do, quick, bring me the broom, we need it in the kitchen, did you put ammonia in your water? Yes? Then put some more." Her confidence in ammonia is absolute, it's true veneration, as if through it she hopes for purification not just of the floor but of the soul as well, as if she herself could be cleansed by ammonia. Because, in a word, she's sick.

Marianne picks up the cash purse behind the bar, sits at a table, and divides the tips in six. Each of them gets enough for a coffee. They know that most of the tip money has disappeared, they've seen bills passing from tables to cash register, which is locked, but no one brings it up because bringing it up wouldn't change the distribution but it would put at risk the only job available. Each of them receives the germ of a tip that avarice has set aside — a piddling amount, a sum that doesn't even show the intelligence that misers often have to conceal their vice. The cook pockets hers with her usual grunt, the *pizzaiolo* says thanks. The dishwasher cries out pompously: "Marianne, darling, I'll take you out for supper," and because he makes her laugh, Grazia warns him about Marco, who's jealous and has a gun.

The night is over. It lasted a year, two years, maybe ten, it lasted a century. If they are able not to think about tomorrow night they're relieved, pleased, ready to sink into sleep where, time and again, full glasses will crash to the floor. At the end of the week, each of them will get his pay — less than half the legal minimum wage — enough for one *Da Nerone* meal and even then without dessert.

Coming home from work around four a.m., Marianne, followed by two scrawny dogs, speeds across the main square and her bike, held together by a single bolt, makes a terrible racket on the uneven cobblestones. She drives along the lake, the animals from the travelling circus, and the moonlight trembling on the water's surface. At night the dark garden is hers, vanished, swallowed up in the heavy floral perfume that the heat preserves, and the spices are all asleep — Luigi, Santa, Giovanni, Alfredo, Illuminata, Fausto, Castissima, the aunt with her cancer and her wig, the great-uncle and his dissolute gaze, *dormono tutti*. Marianne, invisible, exhausted, empty, sits on the doorstep and slowly lights a cigarette, its orange brand burning a hole in the night. The trees shudder above the sloping roof of the shed, she looks for a long time at the smoke rising up to the stars, and listens to the communal spring running under the cement. In a while she'll collect what she needs for watering the flowers and the beans. At four a.m., the water pressure is very high, the watering can fills up right away. In the house, she doesn't turn on any lights. She takes her shower and washes her blouse in preparation for the next day. Then fades away into a deep sleep.

Should we think of work as a secondary activity?

No.

You should work saying yes, more, why not, gladly. To grasp that had taken Marianne several dozen nights of watching the clock whose hand didn't move; of sensing behind the conciliatory words spoken to herself, the rumble of a mixture of hatred and pity, mulling over in vain the possible economic outcome, all of it leading to the oppressive revolt that's shared by the proletariat of the entire world.

Now and then Grazia and Mario have been denounced to the authorities by employees, they've paid fines, Mario without a word, Grazia crying scandal. Never, though, have they been subjected to a surprise inspection, most likely because they know personally whomever it may concern.

The *pizzaiolo* has two children. He lost his job as a bus driver when the company went bankrupt. Since then, he considers himself lucky to spend seven nights a week covered in flour and sweat for a salary that's barely enough to keep a dairy cow alive. He's the only one who smiles all night because, he says, "It beats crying. How about you, Marianne, how's everything, I'm going to make you a pizza, I'll hide it, look, on the top shelf, it's already midnight, and in September, I'll take you to visit Santa Marinella." His eyes betray his

fatigue and his despair, the vague fear that his sons will turn
into anchovies and he himself into an eggplant, and because
that admission passes through his smile as if it were the grille
of a confessional, he gains at once in both modesty and tragic
grandeur.

The cook is sixty-seven years old. She moonlights because
neither her pension nor her memories are enough and because
she's a sturdy, hard-working woman, despite her arthritis.
Her amazing cynicism appears inevitably when fuses blow, as
if her good manners had blown at the same time. One night,
before any customers arrived, Marianne catches her crying
in the kitchen, already exhausted, suddenly too old to be
working in the stifling heat of July and the ovens. Grazia
makes her a *caffè corretto (molto corretto)* with sambuca. The
cook doesn't say thanks, just gulps it down and starts slicing
tomatoes. Her back is broad and her legs are swollen.

Even the village madwoman gets involved. To the great
joy of Grazia, she lives across from the restaurant, hasn't
much to do in the daytime, and doesn't sleep at night. It's
doing her a favour to have her wash the aprons, dishcloths,
rags, and fold the napkins. It brings her prestige, all it costs
is a pizza now and then, and, it's true, a certain measure of
patience to listen as she unburdens herself of existential
concerns shifted onto her trouble with her alarm clock, which
is broken, "*Quando sarà possible, signore, signora, quando sarà
possible farlo riparare, per favore, grazi, signore, grazie signora.*"
The trouble is, her proximity sometimes manifests itself too

noisily in the presence of customers. Luckily, there's a door that opens onto the hill. Luckily, she likes pizza *margherita*. Luckily, there are always dirty rags to keep her busy.

The other waitress is a Scottish victim of an unexpected pregnancy that had confined her to the village ten years earlier. She's thin, dry, rigid, she's a grouch. Her smile looks like a grimace. It's when she curses that you sense she's in fine form, when she sends customers packing without their even noticing.

The dishwasher is studying translation at university. He already speaks three languages in which he imitates Grazia to himself, over the dishwater. It's how he is paying for his studies, a person has to be brave. In the kitchen with the old cook all night long, he applies himself to making her laugh, lavishes on her attention and anecdotes about America, where he's never been and will never go, but that despite the TV news exerts a tremendous fascination over what people think. He might have a chance to improve his lot, but that's not certain either, he's already thirty and has a little belly, for him it's the moment when you topple into either a better life or into too bad, too late: a person has to be brave.

Marianne is only passing through *Da Nerone*. She's from elsewhere, she'll move on, she knows that, they all know that. But observing the *pizzaiolo*, the cook, the madwoman, the dishwasher, and the other waitress trapped here by economic poverty and administrative malfunction, she curses Grazia for the ease with which she profits from the distress of others and still finds a way to complain about the cost of food. When Marianne has gone they'll still be here, busy growing old between the hot ovens, the burning smell of ammonia, and the sick insults shouted over their shoulders.

And so, every night and in spite of herself, Marianne imagines ways to spoil the restaurant's reputation. Insult the best customer, drop a beer down a plunging neckline, sprinkle sand in the salad, steal a third of the forks, take out the coasters that stabilize the tables, refuse a reservation to a group of twenty-five, put water in the red wine, serve a dessert made with cream that's gone bad, pour honey all over the knives. The possibilities are endless, she holds back only because of her concern not to deprive the others of their jobs, mediocre though they may be. Because they won't try to leave, she knows that, the worst thing is that they can't imagine a better life for themselves.

VI

WITHOUT THE WORLD

One morning, throughout the village, word is getting around that during the night the lake has given up the body of a young Swiss woman. Marianne doesn't know if the story is true, but she simply can't go to the lake that day — she is trapped by the cruel notion that, as the first person to swim there every day, she herself might have found the corpse; she is also trapped by the even worse notion that the death could have been intended for her.

On Tuesdays, the central square disappears beneath the market — fantastic, chaotic, noisy, brooms, tablecloths, soaps tossed into upside-down umbrellas, plastic and aluminum jewels, cheese, fish, clothes on hangers like a throng above the throng, fruit, dishes, yarn, leather purses, mailboxes. A fat butcher.

Woodworking tools, beach towels, shoes, chestnut honey, prosciutto, nuts, cleaning products, candies, utensils, coffee makers, fish hooks. Fat, garish women, little gypsies, dogs filled with hope. Marianne wishes she could buy it all.

And then, a month or two later, she realizes that she stays away from the square on Tuesdays, and that when she ends up there by mistake, she only notices the hooks, the empty mailboxes, the young men avoiding their mothers-in-law, the stale food, the swinging purses, the blunt objects, the heat on the honey, the gypsies' eyes — and that the clothes swaying on hangers look like people who've been hanged.

At the very moment when she walks beneath the unmoving clock on via degli Alberi, a mustachioed man stops her to ask the time. Once she has answered him, he keeps staring at her, then asks the inevitable question.

"Are you a foreigner?"

"Yes."

"German?"

"No."

"What?"

"Canadian."

"What's that?"

"I'm from Canada."

"Ah. How long will you be staying here?"

"I don't know."

"You're staying at the hotel?"

"No."

"Where?"

Marianne answers with her usual vague gesture in the direction of her street.

"There?"

"Yes."

"You're Marco's girlfriend."

"That's right."

"Do you know who I am?"

"No."

"His uncle, the brother of his father, God rest his soul."

"Well. Glad to meet you."

"Me too, very glad. Tell me, would you by any chance have a friend as charming as you are to introduce me to?"

"No, I really don't."

"All right. See you next time."

"Yes. Goodbye."

She's still reluctant to say that she is living in the empty house. She knows that by opening it to her, Marco has exposed himself, and she feels the invisible threads that attach her to the four corners of the village, as if the house were also a castle wall, the altar of the church, the Etruscan lake bottom. Marianne never says that she's living in the empty house because it would be false: she is a foreigner who sleeps in Marco's family house, in their village, despite the dead souls drifting in the garden and the live ones that spy on her all day long.

"I live over there," she says invariably, finger pointing vaguely to a place that could just as well be Quebec. "In a little house," she adds for more precision. And if she's asked which one, she gives the street number: three.

After supper, when she wants to let Marco know that she's there, she struggles not to say, "at my place." She says, "over there," "in the little house," then, later, when she realizes that she has nothing to do but wait for Marco, she says quite simply: "You know where to find me."

In the village, everyone knows everything — and nothing — about Marianne. They know that she picked flowers in the garden and through the open window, they can see the bouquet sitting on the table. They know she wears brightly coloured pants, abnormal, and a jacket she really should press. They know that she has sunbathed, how many cigarettes she smokes per day and what brand, and how long she lingers over coffee on the terraces of bars. She sometimes cries out in the night, she has pruned the rosemary; she works at the restaurant on a regular basis; she gets letters from far away, and she reads books in English; she drinks the strongest grappa; she walks to the end of the wharf in the evening; she paints on the street; she sobs in the garden; when she speaks she has the unintentionally erotic accent of a TV commercial; she swims on days when the wind blows strong, and emerges from the water dripping seaweed. They know that she's younger than he is and that he's been more serene since meeting her. They know that the Jeep is rarely parked on the narrow street in the daytime, they know that, and that Marianne is alone in the empty house, in the golden land, all day and even, sometimes, all night.

No one ever inquires about Marianne. No one ever talks to her. They talk about her. They know nothing about her. They know nothing about the distress that gnaws like a rodent at her vulnerable psyche. They know nothing about her language, her friends, about boots squeaking on fresh snow after six months of winter, about her struggle with painting, about her financial woes. They know nothing about the sound of her brother's voice when he phoned to tell her about the birth of his son.

Certain friends rejected by Marco take advantage of her presence nonetheless to renew the friendship. They shout at her in the street, invite her for a meal or a coffee, try to make her talk. They are the faces Marco has warned her about. "Look at that one, he's a son of a bitch, if he talks to you, watch out, lying is as natural to him as breathing." After he's put up that wall of paranoia, the last of the honest men disappears into his intangible work, while she strolls among the sons of bitches.

As for the other members of Marco's family, they only welcome Marianne to the extent necessary to let her know that Marco belongs to them. They are at once Marianne's salvation and her condemnation never to be anything but herself. One day when she's dozing in the garden, she hears her name and looks up. It's the skinny aunt with cancer, who is waving a paper bag through her open window. She says, "This is for you, Marianne, can I come down and deliver it?" "Yes, of course." Naïve, delighted. The bag is overflowing, it's full of plump, ripe figs, the very opposite of the aunt. Marianne thanks her a thousand times and mentions it at lunch the next day. In unison, Marco and his mother exclaim: "Where are they, did you keep them for yourself?" and exchange a look, aghast. Marianne is Marco's shadow on the village streets, a voice that's audible only by standing outside its own discourse, a creature made visible only by her connection to the villagers, and, because of this connection, obliterated all the more.

Marco's mother knows nothing about her either. She sees Marianne at her table nearly every day, notices her weakness for tarts. She asks no questions of either Marianne or Marco, but secretly gathers as much information as she can. What she bought at the market, how long she swam, dear God, she's out of her mind, she'll come down with a terrible cold, did she get enough sleep, did Marco spend the siesta with her, no, he was working, all right, all is well, but what does she eat when she doesn't come here? There is at once courage and cowardice in the way she observes Marianne. The courage to respect her son and to tolerate, unflinching, the village gossip. The cowardice that means not trying to understand Marianne's person and her obvious discomfort. Marianne admires the courage and suffers from the cowardice. But the sloth is shared by the whole village. It's the habit of evaluating human lives against the benchmark of TV soaps. It's the corrosive language that eats away at aging minds and makes them narrower every day.

And that's why Marianne decides she's going to find out how to make the mother laugh. She makes fun of Marco, makes fun of herself. When she laughs, the mother shows her pretty little teeth, her cheeks fill out, and her eyes sparkle through her glasses. Marianne makes her laugh to soften her up, makes her laugh to get closer to her; at the same time giving up on being approached herself — foreigner, thief of sons. She sets herself this modest, trivial goal: at least don't drive anyone away. But in spite of her secret efforts, she ends up lost at the centre of a periphery, a periphery that's deserted and gets wider every day.

If she really thinks about it, each person seems to move about in his own desert. The more she masters the language, the more she can imagine the dullness of these lives that the mysterious depth of their speech had hidden from her. Her neighbour spends all night smoking a joint and playing war games on his computer. When he speaks it's fast, so fast that you wonder when the voice will break into a sob. Mario has been working in his restaurant for ten years now and says he's forgotten what makes up the moments of the day.

A Danish woman, here to look for a man, has been dreaming of leaving for a very long time, she now looks at herself, caught in the web of a couple without a soul and sees clearly that she can no longer move, realizing it while avoiding thinking about it. Uncle Fortunato's job consists of watching the entrances to public toilets, he spends the summer enveloped in human smells while his wife, the aunt with cancer, walks twenty times around the same square, without sitting, without talking, without observing anything on the route she always follows, like a fish in an aquarium, now and then adopting an abandoned kitten that some kid steals from her the next day. A local farmer, tired of seeing people strolling by who swipe his apples, has decided to poison a few randomly, and, randomly, nearly kills his own son. The greengrocer embarks on endless monologues in which he tries to put his finger on the uneasiness he feels when he thinks about women: "I don't have any women to talk to," he says, "sometimes I go to Rome, it's pointless, it's too hot in the car, I sell vegetables, it's what I do, it's all I know how to do, dear God I wish I could speak another language, but I sell fruit, that's the way it is, it takes all my time, it doesn't bring in much money, it means I can't find a woman to talk to who wants more than oranges in the winter." The cousin who delivers fish is expecting his first child and imagines it a male, to be brought up by an English-speaking nursemaid, educated in an American school, freed from the village.

They grow like plants in a pot so old, beneath a sky so blue that they suffer without ever thinking of any possible elsewheres.

I liked the calm on your attentive face, a warm breeze passed over it, and migrating ducks. I was overwhelmed now and then, at brief and precious moments that made all the others fade and that leave me still today — and for a long time yet to come — grateful but removed from everything.

I am a shambles of images huddled one against the other. A red mark between the paving stones of Florence marks the spot where Savonarola was burned. I saw Michelangelo's David, elevated, white, smooth, perfect, nearly triumphant, at once sure of himself and anxious, with a youthful anxiety that no one probably ever sheds. Around him, the Prisoners left deliberately unfinished, bodies trying to escape from the sick stone, eclipsed torsos with no hope of light, straining from the effort to be free, in the infinite task of assuming a shape. There is always the crushing pressure of what is against what will be. Stone is the skin is fear is the weight of everything is the obsession with good and evil where the head is held in both hands so as not to give in to the temptation of sleep.

I would like your perfect blood in mine, your worker ant's mouth on my back, I have stepped, I think, too close to your sun. I wake up with my throat parched, you only exist somewhere else. Your sleep is six hours away from mine, immersed in dreams you believe in with all your heart, but understand nothing about.

One day I walked with you in a sloping field from which we could see the line of the water. The grasses bent to September, you looked at me looking into the distance, I was wearing clothes of yours and the wind blew inside them, onto my white belly, green waves in the trees, the air more and more mauve, and at the end of the fields, an apple tree covered with apples, a fig tree covered with figs, green and purple grapes which you threw to your dogs as if throwing sticks. A ladder leaned against the branch of an olive tree, it pointed towards a moon that seemed to be within reach at the top of ten wooden rungs.

I wake up thirsty, I'm always a little cold, I always know at any moment of the day that we can fly in the toboggan tracks of shooting stars, up against the shivering water that runs from leaf to leaf in the square garden, as if the trees and only they, seeing us finally asleep, were murmuring, happily, our brand-new story. I wake up in the inferno of thirst, drained to the lees by the ravenous memory of your male pleasure, with very little left for me, really very little, enough to say hello, here, now, and to find work around your absence, to fill the time that's on the march and that will save us — maybe, soon, at last — from the other's skin. You exist somewhere else, which is to say nowhere, yet this red fig bursts, red still and always, on my inner walls, as if trying to thank me for having come to you in the land of ripe fruit and uncoiled voices.

If only when we fly the ground never came to meet us, if only we could open our arms like a child who appropriates for himself sea, sky, and vast horizon, with a smile even wider than her arms, happy in the embrace of the world that has come to transport her. If only we'd had every day the power to tumble down the dune, laughing, and the patience to swim as far as the blessed moment when it would become possible to breathe underwater.

"It's time to wash your clothes."

"All right."

"Bring them tonight, at supper time."

"All right."

That night, Marianne brings her clothes.

"Where's the washing machine?"

"Don't worry, I'll take care of it."

"No, no, I'll do it."

"No, no. Put your bag on the armchair, I'll take care of it. Did you bring your sheets too?"

"No."

"It's time you washed your sheets."

"All right."

"It will all be ready tomorrow."

The next day, the clothes are clean, dry, pressed. The mother hands her the bag, saying: "You look ugly in those old pants, you could find some pretty ones at the market for next to nothing if you'd just make an effort."

The following week, Marianne puts up a clothesline in the garden and decides to wash her own clothes by hand.

"I saw your clothesline behind the house."

"Oh."

"It's a bad choice."

"Why?"

"There's no shade. Your clothes will burn."

"There's shade in the morning."

"Then hang them out in the morning."

"Yes. Thank you."

Because of the terrible bareness of her days in the empty house, because of the wandering souls drifting in a landscape made for gods, the terrible question appears in the air which is suddenly, dangerously limpid: why this life rather than another, rather than nothing? Is there a thread to hold onto within sight of a fixed point?

The clothesline itself Marianne gradually comes to see as a rope strong enough to support her own weight, she imagines a fine knot swaying under the living-room chandelier, whole-heartedly offering its meagre embrace. She sits outside and stares at the rope, she sits inside and stares at the void. But her drawings hung on the wall keep repeating the same observation: death is as impossible for you as life because you haven't yet decided anything.

For weeks she wanders around with that dark notion dangling from the end of the rope, and she admires Marco's moral fibre, ruled in his sleep by the diver's costume.

Death was there. I remember, in the empty room of the empty house, I had opened the doors and death was making them beat like a heart about to fail, its arteries all shivering. I was sitting on the floor and I watched her stretch out on the walls, making them crumble even more into plaster dust, I could see my drawings resisting her with all their lines, failing more and more at keeping me alive. I saw the corners of the paper fade, I saw the colour go mouldy. I felt that soon my body would refuse yours, I felt that soon I would hate the language learned for love.

Friendship comes to her now only from fragile presences — dead leaves, dirty glasses, a beached eel, a bare boat, the gnarled trunks of old olive trees, bushes disguised as dust at the side of the road. The grammar of a reasonable life is erased by the first signs of madness. The shutters bang in the night. And Marco's voice resonates all the way to her in moments of presence, but can't save her from what one must experience alone: that nothingness of the self to carry all the way, one tiny step at a time. She becomes a dormant thing at the foot of his love. Unable to leave and unable to stay. She is the unliveable world of the world. Her only work consists of not fearing the depth of the water when she swims, each day farther from the shore.

"Are you hungry?"

"Yes."

"Very?"

"Yes."

"What did you have for lunch? *Qualche panino*? What do

you eat when you don't come here?"

"*Qualche panino.*"

"I see. That's what I thought."

For weeks now she hasn't been going to his place to eat, he hasn't been coming to her place to sleep. It happens repeatedly, as if at regular intervals a wall emerged from the ground and rose up between them, leaving them powerless to connect. During these periods she sits in the garden, motionless, or walks along the lake, endlessly. She waits for rain, which won't come. She waits for Marco who, in his way, might be waiting for her too.

During one of these periods, Marianne hears the garden gate open. Marco knows that she's inside. He walks through the garden, picks up the pruning shears he'd left on the window ledge, then leaves, slamming the gate.

Marco on one side of the window — outside, Marianne on the other — inside; a transparent, normal, clean window, curtainless yet hermetically sealed to their respective states of helplessness. Come back, she wants to cry to him, though she knows that's all it would take to make him disappear for good. An urge to cut all the flowers in the garden, to be outside like him, and also to have the right to a handful of reality, ends up in a gin on the deserted terrace of the hotel — a gin in broad daylight. Ever since the snow, which was already long ago, there'd been no anger. Marianne storms into the bar and breathlessly asks for something to make her feel good. "Iced tea?" "No, gin," she replies in a bass voice, pounding the counter with her fist. The three owners exchange a look. One asks what the problem is, in that typical way of condensing into a single word their countless questions about other people's lives.

"Marco?"

"What, Marco?"

"Where is he, what's he doing?"

"How should I know?"

Marianne picks up her drink, thanks, and slumps into a seat on the terrace. She would have liked this precise moment, this moment of anger, to dissolve into another person's presence, she would have liked to grab hold of a sleeve to keep from departing reality at such breathtaking speed. She looks at her drink. The pulp of a lemon floats peacefully in the gin. Let's drink slowly, she thinks, without other resource. She drinks slowly. The terrace is deserted. She thinks the gin isn't strong enough, it doesn't have the reassuring taste of alcohol. She should have ordered a grappa. She should have brought her cigarettes. She should have stayed in her own country.

Much later that night the garden gate opens again. Marco approaches her, touches her arm, it's his hand, yes, warm, cushioned, and Marianne hates herself for feeling relieved. "How are you, what are you up to, can I take you out for a gelato?" She says yes. A few minutes later she realizes why he has come tonight, preceded by his hand as if by an ambassador.

"I went to the hotel a while ago," he says. "I don't know what you told the women, all three of them laughed at me."

It's confirmed. There is no first aid. They all appropriate the rumour without approaching the pain. She should have taken out a better insurance plan. She should have transformed anger into definitive courage.

VII

NOTHING

Now I would like to write a story with characters, but in such a story I can clearly see that there's only me, you, your dogs and your mother, a little wind, thousands of sunflowers, and the strange time we all flew into, the time of our unmade bed, the time of my emptied life that now, moving backwards, I ought to fill with words that can heal.

I can't.

I must.

Marianne goes to the harbour where the sky is wide, cold, clear, where the moon seems more fragile, more miraculously suspended. The harbour chimes in the wind, the boats moan a little, squeezed against one another just as they are on all other nights. But this night is a night of eclipse. Slowly, it closes its black eyelid over the moon.

And then, slowly, opens it again. At first, only a line, a slender, perfect curve. The sky slips away from the moon, undresses her, clears a path for her; the moon pushes it, struggles to grow from it. Each competes with the other in passivity, apparent or real. In the end, the exhausted star is of a purity never before seen. It punches a hole in the thickness of the dark.

It sometimes happens that monks experience doubt. Their faith departs, with all its belongings, they stay behind, numb, inside the pale structure of their Church, inside its clammy stones. When faith comes home again it is purer than ever, so it's said. Marianne thinks about everybody's night and about her own, about the foolhardiness that sends her deeper every day into the darkness, she thinks about the striking proximity of the absent God as the moon breaks away from the seat of shadow, sets fire, victorious, to the immeasurable, then becomes again the nearest star, there where everything is distant.

Her mistake — there's no mistake: she is simply confronting the danger of living a poem.

We walk alone by the thousands across our little planet, always short of everything, of patience most of all. The eclipse lasts for an hour. Human strength should resemble that regal passivity. When we reach out stubbornly towards a specific point, we neglect to take the necessary detour that will lead us gently to our goal without breaking anything. Marianne spends an hour telling herself that all is lost and that it's good news.

Then Marco comes to look for her with Fulli on a leash, not even glancing at the sky. "It's freezing cold tonight," he says, "let's go for a drink."

When I was a child I built sandcastles on the beach alongside the St. Lawrence. I liked to see the damp sand emerge like a cake from my bucket. I had a red plastic shovel for filling it and for flattening the sand till it was smooth and firm.

I also liked making wells. At two metres from the shore I would start to dig a hole with my hands until I'd reached the point where the river runs under the beach. I liked the pressure of the sand under my nails, I liked its coolness and the way it got progressively wetter till the water came gushing out.

I remember one night. It was towards the end of summer. The river still rose a little at that hour, but I wasn't aware of it yet. Slowly, the water came and touched my shovel. Just as I looked up, a wave enveloped it. When it withdrew I watched, transfixed, as my shovel disappeared.

Frantically, I searched the face of the sand. I found nothing.

I had just seen presence transformed into absence through a mutation that was sudden, unpredictable, irreparable. Red, my shovel — and then, nothing.

The worst thing was the indifference of the vast river, an enemy, its whole gigantic anonymity aimed directly at my toy, its complicity with my beach, it was my helplessness in the face of such a conspiracy. Then I consented to the disappearance of what had disappeared, though something else would never vanish: disappearance itself.

Time drains away by itself as a result of doing nothing. Time is what is shown on the unchanging village clocks. It is truth. The day is at once long and short, it depends on how the eye is drawn to the island's silhouette, to the curve of the wind on the castle tower, and it depends on how carefully we scan the horizon and do only that: stop like the clocks, eyes wide open.

One night around two a.m. a storm wakens Marianne through the open window. Above the roof, the sky cracks like a whip. She goes out, naked inside her raincoat and running shoes. The rain hasn't started yet, but the gravel and the pine needles snap meticulously in the heavy air, waves hurl themselves at the wharf, and as they bump into each other, the masts seem to be sounding an alarm. Marianne goes as close as she can to the water. She watches the storm move all the way around the lake, whet its lightning above the villages as if to curse them, as if to absolve them, and now and then wrap them all together in a wrecked day lasting less than a second.

To have nothing to say. To get up at night and follow the storm, to sleep in the afternoon listening to Fauré, to be at any hour awake or asleep indiscriminately, as long as the body makes no demands. Deduct the night from night and the day from day. Sit in the still garden, decline the rosary of what is necessary, and understand that all has been lost along the way: work, play, friends, everything else.

It feels to Marianne as if she's been living in the village for centuries and inhabiting herself for millennia. In her other life, her active life, measures of time filed past in order of size, as on the pages of a datebook: in the year, months; in the months, weeks; in the weeks, days: Monday, Tuesday, Wednesday, Thursday, Friday, Saturday, Sunday, the days were chronological, each with its hours of light and its hours of darkness, dawn, morning. Noon. Dusk, evening, night. Dawn again. Orderly time, organized time, meaningful time, time that advances: life, deprived of unexpected bursts of fever or rage.

All at once, to board a plane and literally kill time. To advance now only by staying in place, with milk on your lips and a hazelnut to say autumn already, just barely, to say autumn forever, straddling the summer, a cat stretches on the burnt grass and Monday is also Sunday, and morning sleep is just as good as the sleep of nighttime. There's no sidewalk on the avenue of tall pines, their needles carpet the street and cars zigzag through the trees: in the distance, sand from the beach climbs the steps of the hotel and gets into the rooms. It's total anarchy. Anarchy that recalls, beyond timetables and urban layouts, the pact signed by life with itself when inflicting mortality on humans.

Anarchy has come from the desire for a body, for Marco's

body, his body only just removed from the mud, a body advancing beyond languages, like a piece of nature accidentally transformed into human awareness, and covered with the white scars of a life scraped by games with dogs and pleasure with women, by the needles in the undergrowth, the cries of birds shot down in flight. Happiness is fragile, violent, and Marco puts his hand on the wound he himself has committed, to reconcile everything with its brief presence.

Soon, one day, Marianne will return to the schedules of her atrophied city, and gaping inside her will be the valley of dreams. One day, back in reality, she will feel like a bouquet of flowers thrown in the middle of the street. She'll have to muster all sorts of courage to trace within herself the frozen clock's hand, the hand that could mend unstitched time, so she can pay her rent on the first of every month without vanishing entirely against the grey of the city. After Marco, she will try more than anything to protect the space that she has recognized thanks to him, the encroachment of sand into the rooms of the hotel.

I've considered hanging myself from the living-room ceiling, the doors all open, the tramontana would have blown onto my limbs, a door slammed. I'd have unburdened myself of the irksome duty of inventing a meaning. Every time, though, out of respect for the mystery, I've gone out and drawn any little piece of the country struck by shade and sun together. Slowly, so as to be absorbed by them. I was more and more silent. I was moving towards a state of stone, towards a passivity that doesn't even refer to activity as its opposite. Nothing.

I'd gone beyond the stage where it's still possible to secure oneself to reality. I had toppled into the absence of will, attracted more by the fact of falling than of walking. There's a name for that trite state — depression, I think. I would sit in the garden and busy myself with despair at being nothing, sitting on an old canvas chair taken from a garbage can and therefore perfect, worn just enough to be uncomfortable so you won't spend your whole life in it. To be nothing: that's what was still available. Sometimes, in the midst of all that, I would hear you coming — you, your dogs, your offhandedness, your careful ignorance of the desert's extent.

You'd ask:

"What are you doing?"

"Nothing."

"Want to go for a gelato?"

"I haven't got time."

You would smile, I'd get up, fold my chair, I would choose lemon and you, chocolate, you'd complain about work and the thousand things you still had to do, then you'd say: "Well, I'd better be going."

"Okay."

"Where shall I drop you off?"

"Nowhere."

"What are you going to do now?"

"Nothing."

You'd start the Jeep, the dogs would wag their tails, you'd disappear again into your invisible occupations. I would watch you go in a *state of decrepitude that amazed me. Your coming, your going, and on either side — before, after — absence: you were the lifeboat casting me into the sea. No land in sight. I'd walk back, appallingly sluggish, as if between each of my footstep, time rushed in to take a long, an extravagantly long step and in the end, I'd never get to the house, I would sit by the water somewhere and listen to the lake, filled with itself, matching itself. I would close my eyes and only listen, become the slow sound of the waves passing over the dead streets of legend all the way to me, without asking where I lived or where I came from or how long I was going to stay — gratuitously.*

As well as your own, you possessed my destabilized life that you didn't know what to do with. Horrified, I saw the meaning of everything crystallize in your presence and I saw you push away that overly heavy role, it was your lawful right, your legitimate cruelty, I knew that, even as I was sinking into the obsessive hope of once more hearing your car stop at the entrance to the garden.

"German?"

"No. Québécoise."

"What?"

"Canadian."

"Ah, I see! Ah! You're Marco's girlfriend?"

"Yes, I am."

"Where's Marco?"

"I don't know."

"Aha. And how long do you think you'll stay here?"

"No idea."

"I bet he's hunting."

"I couldn't tell you."

"Is that so? Hunting, most likely."

The perfect circle.

The round life of Marco. As airtight as an egg.

The universe on the scale of a village that you never leave. Every face is known, every word predictable.

The lives of those who've decided to be alone. They lack nothing. They are what they are. The lives of those who only work with their hands. Of those who belong to the place where they were born. Geographical contingency brought to the rank of fate: I was born here, therefore I am staying.

Marianne would like to live the contented life of Marco. She would also like to have the wonderful smile given him by the mere sight of a family of ducks. He runs through the rain to count them. His footsteps don't make a sound on the ground. They are the ground. He enjoys everything. His everything consists of very little.

Already, Marianne has travelled too much, read too much. The wind introduces into her hopes and desires for justice. Nothing is ever enough for her. She pictures her life nowhere, she wishes it were everywhere. She is cold then in the opening of possible worlds. She would prefer a life like Marco's, a round, closed world, a perfect circle. She would prefer not to ask for anything.

Now and then he gets into his Jeep. Drives along the main road, turns left without signalling, the left being, as he says, his natural tendency; he drives along the lake, goes home. Back to square one. The meal is ready. He eats, it's good, he's content.

At first, Marianne has the illusion that she's entering Marco's egg and looking for her place there. She has the illusion that she is modest. She believes that a modest place in a closed egg will be enough for her too. But it's Marco's egg. Others don't enter it. He doesn't need anyone. Besides, it's too small. Too small for two to fit. To tell the truth, even if she were alone she wouldn't fit.

I looked for you in your perfect life.

You are, with no object, no adverb, and because of that distinctiveness no preposition will ever join us.

To come close to you and through your silence, slowly and painfully come back to myself, to return to my more succinct reality, to my dullest name, you said that by dint of saying nothing: be.

Behind the three windows of the empty house, I was incapable of surviving the brutal fact of being alive, of being naked inside my life. Behind the three windows and the two doors, time became boredom, boredom became hatred, hatred became destruction, and there was that terrible choice on the ground, in the very spot where, on the first night, you'd flung the mattress: madness or a plane.

I think about the way you walk, upright, on the wet rocks — for a long time I believed every word. From far away I remember everything and even more, of what — beneath things said, done, and seen — would give to my soul a body and to my heart, a heart.

These weren't a few months of my life: they were a few months of my death. Now, on every Quebec morning, I have trouble believing that it was me — that broken thing on a floor without furniture, that object laid down there by lightning, totally burned, scarcely able to repeat to itself in a low voice: don't worry, it will all work out, and then: but go away, what are you waiting for, go tomorrow, tonight, disappear as fast as you can. That thing driven back day by day into waiting passionately for the sound of your car and the palm of your hand, sleeping an infant's sleep in your hair: it was me.

I was that thing. It can take years, to heal someone from lightning.

I've also seen fatigue draw new, indelible wrinkles on your face, I've seen you suddenly tired, tired of everything, and in a very short time, I've seen your forehead move farther back in your hair, seen more grey in your hair and, one night when I asked you if it was because of me that you were aging like that, I heard you answer: Yes, smiling, yes, I think it's you who is making me age so much.

The worst thing is fatigue. Fatigue comes from burns that you don't go near, to which you fail to say: hello, glad to meet you, here you are. Fatigue comes from the hole an airplane carves in the blue of the sky, between the houses of my city. Maybe you never existed: fatigue comes from doubt about your existence. Maybe I dreamed you. Fatigue comes from the wreckage of a dream.

It comes from the pointlessness of everything that isn't you.

I met you in a shudder and that's how I come back to myself, with teeth chattering without being cold, with sangfroid, without a hint of fear. No one sees the floating debris that I can feel bumping into me on all sides. Someday, perhaps, to remember only happiness and to think with gratitude about the movement of your hand across the eyelid of my life. And then, quietly, to move my own hand over my warm eyelid and find myself safe from vertigo.

There are other planes for other countries. There are the voices, the hands, of other men, there are other men. But there is you, and your ashes under everything. There is your lost voice, your lost hands, there is you, lost. There is me who has flown away, enraged, exhausted.

Here.

Certain exuberant flowers. One of them, settled comfortably inside its pinky-orange, maybe even yellow, vibrant in its indecisive garment, pure poem to watch being picked, it will start out at eight o'clock on its way to the cemetery where Marco's father lies, dead from cancer, from alcohol, from a bitterness never resolved by his family, his grave tirelessly adorned with flowers by the mother who, when he was alive, couldn't stand his presence.

The flowers may explain why, so early in human history, this land was chosen for making children. Perhaps the flowers are themselves those children — who became adults, and then corpses stored in Etruscan chambers covered with earth, transformed into mountains that archaeologists now disassemble with tweezers and government grants.

In this region, the oldest graves are shaped like an inverted uterus. A narrow corridor leads to it, widening towards the inside. Preparation of the burial chamber, dug with a pick, goes on for a good part of the life of the person it's intended for. When the time comes, the deceased is laid out on a bed, along with some precious objects. The gravediggers then leave, sealing it shut. Memory is condemned. They hide the door by reconstructing the mountain in front of it. One does not visit the dead. They are allowed to go to their better life, they're entrusted to the care of the earth, heads turned towards the most beautiful horizon. Once sealed, death is invisible, irretrievable, it is dead. Over the millennia and unbeknownst to them, people will picnic in front of those gates to the beyond.

Marco's mother puts flowers on her husband's scrupulously Catholic grave. The stone bears his name and the dates of the two ends of his life. He too they put in a hole, but without losing track of him. You go to the cemetery, you lay flowers on his grave, perhaps with some tears and, more rarely, some words. With a certain fatigue about the nothingness of life. His possessions are distributed to his friends and immediate family, which inevitably leads to disputes: they aren't enough to complete unfinished sentences, to alleviate doubts, and to say aloud what was essential. A tobacco pouch: practically nothing. You'd have had to snatch the time for love from ordinary time. You'd have had to do it during life so that life would be filled with itself, and death would take nothing important, practically nothing, a soul that has already passed into the hoop of love.

My father told me about a Breton farmer who one night assembled his whole family, including the children. He said simply that he was going to die, and then he died, simply, at the end of his simple life, he died a death called natural and in that way similar to all other deaths, even those of insects.

One night Marianne and Marco arrive so late that the mother has opted not to fix a meal. They decide to go to the restaurant. It's cold and the moon can't quite move up from the horizon of the fields. The road is long. Straight. Marco drives fast. All at once the vague shape of an animal looms before them. Marco switches lanes to avoid it. Then brakes and backs up. In the headlights the shape reappears: it's a dog, he's lying there on his side, motionless. "*Dio,*" Marco mutters (no one will ever know if he swore or if he saw the divine move across the broken body). "I think he's dead," says Marianne. Marco doesn't respond. He leaves the car in the middle of the road, headlights levelled at the poor heap. He walks towards it and, sensing his approach, the dog opens his eyes bright with fever, raises his head, incredulous, as if to say, "No, it's impossible, did you stop because of me?"

Marco crouches down. "Where does it hurt, *poveretto?*" he asks, feeling the dog. "Oh! You're all broken inside, we'll take you to the side of the road, come on now, come on." Delicately, as if he were handling pick-up sticks, he tries to lift the dog. The animal moans and quivers, you can see his terror-stricken heart throbbing under his skin. "Wait." Marco runs to the car for a newspaper, slips it under the dog, squeezes its muzzle in his hand. "When a dog is in pain it may bite without meaning to." While he's dragging it to the side of the road, the dog looks at Marianne with heartbreaking, fiery eyes, the eyes of the dying.

He lays it down in the wet grass. "His spine is broken, we ought to finish him off, but I can't do it." He takes a rope from the car and fastens it to a fence-post, "in case he gets up and crosses the road," thinking this might give the dog a hope, a very slim hope, of being free to walk and to be tied up because he's free. Yet after stroking and petting him for a long time, he tells him the truth. He says to the dog: "You have to die tonight, it's too bad but that's the way it is."

At the restaurant, during half the meal Marco tries to contact a veterinarian who'll agree to come to the road and euthanize the dog. One says yes, for an exorbitant fee. Marco comes back to the table, furious and discouraged, picks at a little wild boar. His beautiful eyebrows are frowning, you can see the wrinkles that are there when he looks his age.

"Why," he asks suddenly, "why were we the ones to meet that dog? Why do things like that happen to me? Listen, that upsets me, a lot."

"You're the only one who stopped. The dog had resigned himself, you could see. A dozen other cars must have gone by before us."

"They all thought, 'Too bad,' and kept on driving. Even the son-of-a-bitch who hit him."

"Maybe that's why we drove there. It's far, it's late. Everything worked out so that you were the one who took the trouble to help that dog."

"Mmm."

They eat a little, don't talk.

"But maybe it's actually the opposite," says Marianne after a moment.

"What?"

"Maybe it was to help you that we met that dog."

"Why me?"

"So that you could be with a dying dog."

"Sure, me, who lost two bitches this year, thanks a lot, that's enough."

"You lost your bitches but you still haven't accepted the fact that you've lost them."

"So?"

"You couldn't even watch them die."

"So what?"

"So, maybe that dog was a chance for you to be with a dying dog."

"Come off it."

"Maybe it was to help you accept it."

"I don't want to accept it. Okay, Peggy was old, it's normal to die, but Ambra — that, you see, I cannot accept."

"You have to let them go now. That's all you can do for them."

"You're telling me I'm possessive."

"I'm telling you it's hard to let them go."

Marco pushes away his plate, crosses his arms. Marianne tries to pour him more wine, he puts his hand over the glass. They skip dessert.

On the way home, along a stream of fields that are all alike, Mario spies the post where the dog is attached and stops. He gets out with his flashlight. The dog was waiting for them, right away his feverish eyes focus on them, you can see that he has just one hope: not to die tonight. Because of his broken spine, his rear has dropped into a cavity in the ground and his torso is horribly twisted. Marco gently puts his paws back in their normal position and pushes him away from the cavity so that he'll "die the way you're supposed to die: good and straight."

He starts talking to the dog. Marianne is holding the flashlight. In its circle are the creature's eye, his neck straining with effort towards the voice, the two of them alone in the big, unjust world. With regret, Marco concludes: "Safe journey."

He sighs, stands up, gets in the car, starts it. Then flinches slightly, as if he's forgotten some detail. He stops the engine. Gets out of the car, undoes the rope, and takes it with him. "He'll die free, that's the least we can do for him."

Early one morning a scarf of mist was drifting across the lake between the beach and the hill; I held my head on the water's surface while dawn was undressing the shore. I was doing the breaststroke and every time my head emerged, the scarf was there, receding towards a deeper peace, a more tenacious wound, slowly allowing the appearance of a tree, of two houses perhaps — allowing daytime life to begin. That's the only definition of the soul that I've come up with, long after you asked me the question.

VIII

ETERNITY

The way I feel is strange, strange because you'll never know it, because you'll never see the bedroom opened by the sound of your footsteps, or the lightness of the veils that hang there waiting for you, or the blood burned during that waiting, or my bare feet set free from it, and because you'll never have in your ear the sound of your own voice when it told me words that I didn't understand yet, that I took to be jewels gone astray on their way to a princess and dropped in front of me with troubling grace. My strange feeling I brought along on my journey, sometimes we stopped at your place, for a while, I don't remember how many months, we were like beggars outside your house, and though you pretended to recognize us, you ignored us, and even as you were greeting us, you sent us away, I took my feeling with me intact, strange, and I've pulled it all the way here, to this page of writing where it is looking for a side where it can finally stretch out.

I can't find the missing word. I write relentlessly, perhaps in search of that word, of the kiss that would waken my mad hope and make it legitimate, the word that would have made it right for me to leave, to wait for you and to sink in so deep.

We often say "love" to justify such madness, to give it an acceptable face, to give it back to the concrete daily life from which it can only escape. "Love" is the word invented to name a hole punched in reality. But we do not know the love of others, we know others only through the love we make with them, never through its green kernel, because it belongs to them. "Love" is not the word I'm looking for.

I may perhaps be looking for your name, different from the one you were christened. The name of your quiet strength, of your fragility, of the closed kingdom where they speak language of beasts. I am looking for the new name for the self I lost along the way just as I had finally grasped the slippery edge of my soul, and was imprinting my odour in the memory of your dogs.

I have nothing but writing to help me try to invent a word that won't exist but that eventually, as after an eclipse, would shed its light on the road we grope along at night, so close to the sky. I was the outstretched horizon a child runs towards, arms flung open, and then, broken, a fragment of a return to the familiar country, to my mother tongue and the grey duty of days that are all alike.

I still have no comprehension of what happened. If I could find the word I'm looking for I might be able to separate you from the source of all joy.

The western world once spent a summer glued to its TV to follow the story of a child who'd fallen into an artesian well. This was in the early 1980s, it was headline news in all the papers. For days, they tried desperately to get the child out. Finally he died — of starvation, thirst, cold, and fear.

I played outside, thinking about him all day, thinking about his legs wedged in the well. I might even have prayed to the good Lord for him once or twice before I fell asleep, just in case. I grew up. Often, for no reason, I thought about him, thought again about his fear and about how slowly death had crept to him.

I found out recently that all this happened a few kilometres from your village.

In your mother's house the TV was always on, and when I glanced at it there was nothing but blood and bottle-blondes. You were the king of the remote control. You'd adjust the volume, switch channels, and tell us to be quiet when some news item interested you. On one exceptional night, I took the control. An American movie had just started. It began with a mother and her three children playing in an ordinary suburban backyard. The phone rings. The mother answers. When she returns the swing is swaying back and forth and there are only two children. The mother calls to her youngest, who doesn't reply. She calls again, her voice more and more anxious. Then she looks at the other two who are standing, dismayed, in front of a pipe that's planted in the ground. She gives them a questioning look, not daring to voice the burning question. They look back at her, pathetic, not daring to express the absurd reply to her unspeakable question. The mother bends over the well and calls again. From down below comes a moan, a sob, the feeble, hollow voice of oblivion.

The baby has fallen down the hole.

The film was inspired by a true event, something that happened in the United States and therefore has a happy ending. It takes several days to get the child out of the well. The channel is too narrow for an adult. It's a baby-sized hole. A parallel well is dug. The stone is unyielding. A geologist is brought in, who uses stainless steel drill bits, advancing a few centimetres an hour. The tension is extreme, the child is dehydrated, the mother is comatose, the father wants to beat up the entire world. People crowd around the tragedy, dozens of individuals come to suggest solutions for this never-before-seen problem, they dig, dig, men come back out of the hole half-asphyxiated, their skin grey. They heat the well, the nights are cool, a mike is sent down to keep track of the child's heartbeats, her mother sings songs to her, if she falls asleep even for a moment, there's panic.

I was glued to the TV and your mother, amazed at my sudden interest, watched me watching the movie. In the end, the baby is saved, the crowd applauds, the ambulance takes off, the music explodes: this is America.

That night I let you sleep alone and I walked back to the empty house.

We are interested in mysteries, we would like to see what isn't shown, we'd like to know what can't be known. First, we study philosophy, which goes on for a few years, then, with no idea of what to do, we become aware of the silence of books. We allow ourselves to be called by obscurities more obscure than those of language, we try to find *them among the desire of skins and cosmic cycles. We're fascinated by disappearance, the disappearance of objects and of our own selves, the disappearance of daylight. We dig. After all, it's to find water that we dig wells. We pass through a canal to be born and so we try to find a canal where we can repeat that act, one that will renew us; we glide into the well expecting we'll be able to get out, but we remain stuck there, and suddenly the expected birth has a terrible similarity to death.*

I was ashamed of my body in your overly narrow streets. I had packed in my suitcase lightheartedness, curiosity, enough strength to part with everything; but none of that would have sufficed without blindness. Blindness and the terrible beauty of blindness, the dream of being happy and blind, happy as a blind person, miraculously refreshed by the opacity of your universe, resolute, complete, squeezed between your lake and its hill. I dreamed of freedom from the exhausting responsibility to clearly distinguish one thing from another, and to decide at all times which was good and which bad. And that's how we fall down a well, I think, it's fairly simple, once you've broken with the day and made a deal with the darkness of the poor verb "to love."

In September I extended my courage to take better advantage of your country's light. It was a light like gold bullion, I remember it had the exact temperature of the body, and by circulating inside it one felt omniscient. I knew though that I was going to leave, that the time foreseen in advance, foreseen from the beginning, would arrive.

*I was alone in that story, which would end the way it had started —
fabulous and sad, with veins like the veins in marble and in the
migration of birds. The wind lengthened the street in early evening,
made it Gothic, there was a smell of fire, and its way of clouding the
distance; it was your autumn, I had to wear a scarf and a jacket, at
night you pulled the blanket over us. I stepped into your autumn,
fascinated, and the lake was higher and higher and the sky full, and
full like the sky were the hunters' rifles; I understood that your
autumn wasn't mine and that, as I was stepping into it with surprise,
I was all the more foreign to it. Every day, I was refused facts that
should come on their own, of no interest to you but brand-new to me:
that light, for example, and that wind. I entered without entering
among you. Everything told me, laughing: farewell, already. Caressing
you, I placed upon you airport and suitcases, your desire left on the
shelf and my memory haunted by the weeds in the lake. I stepped
into your autumn, it was one more moment that knit us together, the
final moment before my own white winter, and then all winters —
in another country. In that country, mine, which would no longer be
mine absolutely, which would simply be just one more country, a
country to live one's life in, a life like any other, a life without yours.*

*And so before I boarded the plane, I decided to try at least once
to take another trip. I left for Assisi and as soon as the train started
up, I realized that I was intact, really, that I was myself, that I was
able to step outside the perfect circle.*

Assisi is a rose-coloured town where the sun becomes a great
mystic strolling along walls and steeples. White passages rise

between houses, blue vines drop from the roofs, delinquent fountains of coolness hide in shady corners. The eye is suddenly naked, as if it were new, it is the round eye of the newborn gazing at a world not yet touched by evil. In Assisi there soars, suspended, the possibility that God exists.

Access to the Basilica of St. Francis is by a kind of ramp that blends into the city walls and from the top of which one looks out onto the dusty plain. During the thirteenth century the Basilica, built to the glory of Francis recognized by the Church, had been the subject of a controversy between those who wanted something grandiose and those who endorsed Franciscan asceticism. The two were reconciled by erecting a vast, elevated basilica and under it, a squat crypt devoted to the worship of the holy remains.

In the upper basilica, Giotto painted the famous cycle that recounts the life of Francis *ad infinitum*. His blue is different from anyone else's, similar perhaps to that of a pair of scissors we had as a child and later on lost, along with the pleasure of our Sunday games. Around the characters, architectures whose groping perspective is reaching for the Renaissance without losing its medieval naïveté — they are talking, leaning towards people's gazes, all gazes; those of visitors and those of Francis himself, of his friends, of the pope. Sometimes they stay balanced in the hand of a single man.

Behind Giotto, in the transept, his master, Cimabue, is dying. The frescoes now have no colours but those of the earth, they are on their way to the place of their own origins.

They expose, shamelessly, human ambition, they prefigure the painter's own lingering death, its subjectivity hanging on the wall like a respirator, but still beseeching, still celebrating, still. The still soul of Cimabue. Furtively, Marianne snaps a couple of photos when the guard's back is turned. She is well aware that she should let time pass even over fragile things and protect them no more than a maple tree in autumn.

The small basilica is low. Display cases hold Francis's clothing, starched and mended — his sandals, his nightdress — ridiculous without him, without his charisma and his passion. The dead should be allowed to die, the frescoes to withdraw, we should inhabit as best we can without trying to possess.

From the first night, in a sense, I was quite certain that all times are in fact a single time, round and full, and that I would travel forever down the muddy dirt road, with your face on my left, the storm in the windshield, and that strange smile which seemed to say thank you, *but also:* I've always known that you would come to me. *You drove eternity like a nail into ordinary time. I had the impression I was opening my consciousness with forceps in order to make it capable of a fourth dimension wherein we would be eternal. I had the impression that what I was opening had always existed, that I had simply understood a phenomenon that's never explained to us because it is inexplicable, one to which perhaps only spirits drifting towards a last resort gain access. I understood that not only is eternity possible but that it has long since arrived on its own, open for us in* advance like a big house where the door hinges don't even creak, are always new and oiled, always ready to move.

What I understood about time was also a form of serenity, a sublime form of serenity, a reconciliation not only promised but already sealed, for a long time, forever. Patience, an art I'd been absorbed in mastering for such a long time, suddenly struck me as useless; it only served to project into the future something that was already present and, at the end of the day, despite its good offices, we finally miss out on everything. On the very first night, the car drove into the storm and instead of being afraid, I was not afraid.

The assurance of eternity: I should be able to choose it over nostalgia, but also over hope.

Long afterwards, later, now, once I was back in my slowly moving winter, with its sky higher than others and its ever-present crackling and creaking, I also understood that not only was I still on the dirt road, but that I was all the more present there, as my calendar moves away from that date, as events continue to happen and to happen elsewhere, as if to the exact degree that the passing of time invalidates eternity, eternity is somehow deepened. It's a strange paradox, a paradox similar to your strange smile — and strangely enough, I'm no longer suffering at all, I've decided to take everything on board: you alive, you erased and myself alive in the thought of you and in other thoughts, in the thoughts that pass and then come back — or not.

I'm not talking about memory. Memory I also have, sharp, precise, with the breath of the wet countryside, the muffled sound of tires in the mud and that of the engine that was always threatening to break *down. Memory is a trace of the past, it is present as representation. When we try to relive an experience by gathering together all its components, even if it's just to see a film again, we are always disappointed, because the component that has become memory will never be given back. Memory is flat, thin, fragile, it is under construction and in the process of disintegrating; memory is banal because it is just a product of our mind, and our mind is always poor. Memory is like the Signorelli fresco in the last chapel on the right in the Duomo of Orvieto. To see it at close range, I climbed onto the scaffolding; work was underway at great expenditure of gold leaf to prevent the fresco from disappearing. Inside its new skin, though, it was disappearing, it was settling into the stone of the walls, but that, they never mention. Recollection is something like that scaffolding, memory is like the restored fresco: it's the new skin applied to the past in order to bear its disappearance which is always, in the end, our own. I like memories, but I fear illusion.*

Eternity is not like memory. Eternity is the fact that once a fresco has been sunk into the wall and once the wall has eroded to the ground, it is still intact and close to me, despite my ignorance of them, despite my absence. Eternity has no need of me, yet I am part of it all the same. Eternity contains the gulags, the death camps, the Academy of Athens, the Etruscan necropoli, it holds prehistoric fingermarks, the American flag planted on the moon, your birth and your first tooth; it holds my sister, who is crying because she thinks her hair is too short when she catches her reflection in a car window while my mother is clasping her hand on the way home from the hairdresser; it holds my brother, who is changing a diaper, it holds my father, who is looking for wood to carve: we are all there, the dead and the living of all times and all ways of being; your mother was born, she lived, and she will die inside the village perimeter, I want to travel around the planet, that hardly matters in the face of the fact of existing and, especially, in the face of the fact that within our own existence there is everyone else's. And that which we no longer are and that which we have not yet become, we are already.

She's sitting in a bar and would like to write to someone, she hasn't yet decided to whom; the paper is in position, already a little stained with coffee and a roll. A man is looking at her, as other men do, but unlike the others he comes up to her and bends over to ask in English: "Are you a writer?" He has on a white hat beneath which his black eyes glisten like the back of a cricket.

"Not really," she replies.

"Maybe you will be some day." He pulls out a chair and sits down.

"We'll see."

"Are you travelling on your own?"

"Yes."

"That's good. Where do you come from? Germany?"

"From Quebec."

"From what?"

"Canada."

"Ah! America! I went to New York once. It's wonderful, New York. I love cities. Do you work?"

"Very little."

"You watch people."

"That's right."

"If you're a writer, you know, looking around you is a full-time job."

"Are you a writer?"

"Yes. Do you read a lot?"

"Yes."

"What do you read?"

"Whatever."

"Do you like tragedy?"

"A lot."

"Do you think it resembles you?"

"Yes, I do."

"Comedy's better."

"Maybe."

"Love tragedy, but choose comedy."

She bursts out laughing. The men at the next table turn around and prick up their ears. They don't understand English ("What language are they talking?" "German, I think." "Ah, yes, I recognize it now.") but they're listening attentively. One of them, thin and stooped, sends Marianne suspicious little signs.

"What's your name?"

"Marianne."

"I'm Angelo. Do you like to travel?"

"A lot."

"Good. And you like to write."

"Yes."

"You ought to live in your own house, you know."

"That's not easy."

"No. A person has to find their own house and live in it, but keep a window open to let in the world."

Marianne doesn't reply. She's looking at Angelo. Suddenly, behind the brim of his hat, she catches a glimpse of his wings, transparent. Angelo realizes that she has seen them and he smiles as well. New suspicious signs from the man at the next table.

"Remember, now," says Angelo. "Choose comedy and don't forget the window."

Marianne puts away her paper scattered with the crumbs and with Angelo's words, words as white as the backs of crickets. She gets up, pays for her breakfast and Angelo's coffee, which he lets her do while the bartender looks on, incredulous.

Angelo leaves. The man at the next table steps up and cranes his neck towards Marianne so that the ligaments stand out: "Not talk with him, is crazy, crazy," he declares sententiously.

"*Grazie del consiglio*," she replies. He smiles at her and retracts his neck, satisfied with the impact of his intervention. She picks up her purse and leaves. On the street the wind of Assisi is blowing and, as soon as she's out the door, Marianne feels the newborn feathers of her wings moving on her back.

She runs into Angelo a few hours later; he's busy writing on a typewriter as he sits astride the wall of the fortress, he is writing in the open air, the way the Impressionists painted, and she doesn't stop to say hello because he seems to be absorbed, but even more because she assumes he won't recognize her. That he was intended to pass by her only once, a light above that of the day, just one time to moisten her wings and give them, as we do to a swing, the push they need.

The traveller is intact. Only his shoes deteriorate. He is entering the country of others, he sometimes imagines, simply for the pleasure of giddiness, that he will stay there for his whole life, but the next day he's off again, his life is elsewhere because it is everywhere. The traveller has a name, the one on his passport. In other languages, he's often asked to repeat it, people pronounce it incorrectly, always, it's the name of a stranger, the traveller is a stranger.

At the best of himself, in the root of his eye, the traveller is intact. The journey takes place outside him and new faces, unfamiliar tastes, the colour of the houses merely consolidate that which he already was. As what is known is dispersed, he notes that, enriched with new images, he is more and more simply himself, more and more stripped of the superfluous that we accumulate when we stay at home, more and more poor in the poor eyes of normality, yet more and more independent, as he has fewer resources.

If he can walk, the traveller walks. He watches places parade before him that don't belong to him, with houses to which no one invites him. Fountains are friendly because their users are anonymous. The traveller bends down, wets his hair and drinks some water, sits for a moment and then sets off again.

The traveller sets off again. The journey, he knows, is merely a metaphor for his own life, for everyone's life, a metaphor for life itself: with no other content than that — the space between. He lacks the time to grow attached to anything, he carries no heavy objects. He has only his two legs, only his thinking, and his thinking improves day by day, as landscapes open in him the gate to a cloistered consciousness, a consciousness that's waiting for a key for itself. The traveller's heart waits calmly for the journey, the way a puppy waits for us to find a name for him, without even thinking about it, already prepared to respond as soon as he is called.

At a hotel I met a Dutchman living in England who had decided to walk in the Italian mountains for four months. He had hesitated for a long time before choosing the book that he'd bring with him. In the end he opted for poetry because he could reread poems a number of times. I asked him what he missed most while he was walking. He told me, Music, I think. That night I lent him some music that he could listen to in his room. He was gone the next morning. He'd left the music on my doorstep, along with the book of poems.

The traveller doesn't burden himself with anything. After a moment, he realizes that he no longer burdens himself even with himself, that he himself is stuck to his own footsteps in a manner so tranquil that it scarcely weighs a thing. He realizes that he is becoming what he always was, without a doubt: a footstep.

Because he knows that he will leave no matter where he is, he keeps himself in a state of perpetual mourning that is less and less painful, that at times even makes him happy. That's because the state of mourning is also a state of wakefulness, as are real funerals. It is a state of exacerbated wakefulness and during it the traveller accompanies things until the next moment, imminent, when they will disappear. The traveller is like a person who chooses the wrong door and ends up in the room of a dead man. He greets the corpse, telling it at the same time hello, delighted, goodbye, farewell, knowing at once that he has arrived at a corpse that has already embarked on decomposition, but is trying nonetheless to make his acquaintance. The worlds the traveller visits are these: they are worlds that have been embedded in their own habits for a long time, motionless worlds where the inhabitants keep watch with more or less energy, attention, and singular patience. The traveller enters there one day, he sees them for the first time, and because of his new way of seeing, still capable of astonishment, worlds light up in their slightest details.

Should it happen that the traveller stops and settles down, that he ceases to be a traveller, little by little the worlds die out and are covered with dust. The traveller finds a hook for his coat, buys himself a cooking pot and some cushions. In each of the objects he acquires, he will deposit a fragment of his soul, in his consciousness he will open only doors already open, and soon he will only be astonished that he's no longer astonished, by anything.

She gets on a train and gets off at the station nearest the village. Marco was supposed to meet her. He's late. By the fountain where she had waited for him when she came back from France, she is waiting for him again. It seems to her that few ingredients have been added to their love story between these two times of waiting, as if waiting, linking all these moments together, has finally made them only one — one long moment spent at the train station.

He turns up late and unsmiling. He takes her to the village. It's the first night of the Fish Festival. Between the pine trees, long tables at which the whole province has come to feast. Above the tables, a huge fishing net. Marco and Marianne, sitting side-by-side, have already been separated by the frescoes and the friction of the rails, the wings in the wind of Assisi and the wear and tear of her sandals, they're already far apart from one another at the moment when, at the fish table, she decides never to end up like them, with a net hanging over her head.

IX

THE BROKEN CIRCLE

During the night of September 26, 1997, Marianne and Marco are sleeping together and they don't wake up. The epicentre is in Foligno, a town near Assisi. In less than ten seconds Cimabue comes crashing down. His slow fading ends rather brutally — in a thousand pieces on the floor of the apse. Frescoes live for seven hundred years. We think that they'll bury us all, along with our grandchildren. We visit them once, their beauty scalds us. Twenty days later they crumble into dust. There's nothing to be said. It's the end of an image. It marks the true death of the painter, much delayed. We rarely hear the pulsation which marks the fragility of all things, especially that of stone. Two priests lie dead beneath the rubble; dozens of people left homeless couldn't care less about the fate of a fresco. But experts examine Giotto and are waiting for news as one might wait for news from a friend with heart disease.

The next day, something new. It's not even the echo of the first tremor, it's a second earthquake. The destabilized houses finish crumbling. The vault of the basilica collapses in a huge cloud, in front of the trembling cameras that were examining Giotto as if with a stethoscope. Television shows it happening continually, in slow motion. The vault collapses. So much patience reduced to nothing. But Giotto is intact.

In ten days, maybe sooner, Marianne will have left the village.

Walk alone, you said, get by without me.

The last days, I only perceived metaphors of my own distress, the worn skin of fruit, the icy about-face of the lake under the tramontana, the furious four-hour storm, the pine tree bowed down with its head in the water, cheeks drained of fading flowers, the weeping of willows, dog excrement on the walkway in the harbour, the curses of an empty-handed fisherman, the islands mired in mist, the barricaded hotel, the missing hand on the statue of Christ, out-of-tune scales, weeds, power failures, nets stretched on the beach.

The earthquake in Assisi, the houses in shreds, and Cimabue swept into a dustpan by some tearful lovers of medieval art.

The sighs of Fulli, who wants to play outside, your own sighs, devoid of any instructive word, those of the empty house with its crumbling plaster when the terrible shadows of noonday ghosts pass over it.

When I arrived in your country I had an unshakeable trust in the vaults of churches. Trust remains: more fragile, it becomes trust in the effort made by vaults of churches to resist earthquakes. As for what's possible: I only trust the vault of prayers surviving that of churches.

I passed among you, who are motionless. I trust only my own footsteps, beyond the walls, towards the horizon glimpsed as I learn to lean on my steps themselves.

It's anger that saves her. All at once it becomes impossible to mask it with distress, to put it to sleep in the afternoon, to bury it under the beauty of a body. Anger rises. Cold anger, anger like the sinew of angers, the pure force of one who only wants to live. Anger, one day, suddenly, does away with expectation.

It's afternoon, everything is closed, but the grimy café at the corner of via degli Alberi sells cigarettes at this time of day, she knows that, she also knows that they sell the strongest brands. She buys a package, smokes three, one after the other. The square is deserted and with no cars, no humans, no shadows, it seems immense, its cobbles shrink back to the roots of the roofs, the sun overwhelms everything with the same torrid colour, it obstructs windows — a killer. Marianne heads for the only telephone that works. She's going to call the airline. She will tell them: I have to leave here. Crossing the square, she hears a man's voice behind her, a voice that's calling Sabina and is aimed directly at her, there's no mistake, there's no one else. Marianne turns around. A man all in leather gets off his motorcycle and makes his way to her. He smiles. "Are you Sabina?" "No," she tells him, and he looks disappointed.

"I'm trying to find Sabina," he explains, "and you look like her."

"And who's Sabina?"

"A girl I loved seventeen years ago."

"And then?"

"We haven't seen each other since. I was in the area and we'd arranged to meet here, today, to get together."

"And I resemble her."

"Yes, you resemble her, but you aren't her. Where are you from?"

"Canada."

"Canada?"

"Yes. And I'm leaving tomorrow."

"Will you be away long?"

"Forever."

He falls silent. Marianne puts her hand on his arm the way the locals do and wishes him good luck with Sabina. He smiles and wishes her a safe trip. She walks to the telephone, he sits on a bench, the square is deserted, and Sabina doesn't come.

Actually, thinks Marianne, he did recognize me. I'm a forerunner of Sabina, here in the desert of the central square, from now on I am Sabina, who's come here to look for the face that changed her life seventeen, twenty-five, a thousand years ago, and at this moment, there is no difference between my soul and the square, only the unbearable similarity between one desert and another, both of them without shadows or humans — deadly.

Leaving this country, she knows that she's about to enter another that is even more cruel, the country of fascination and absence — absence that's connected to the being and that time fails to fill, even after it is cured of the absence of the body, of speech, of laughter, even after it is cured of all the rest.

When Marianne announces to Marco that she's leaving the next day, his face mobilizes, impassively, all his right angles, but Argo, in the garden, starts to cry. Marco pets him and the more he pets the dog, the more the dog cries. Marco looks up at Marianne and tells her, with a big grin: "He's a very sensitive dog." Then immediately lowers his eyes.

Perhaps the desire for God emerges like that, with a sudden aware-
ness of time that condemns us to lose small things — the red shovel,
a billfold, some gloves — and then the important things — a
friend, my grandfather, and summer, several times. A struggle against
loss, the desire for a thread that can bring together the passing of
everything and hold it in its invisible hand like a bouquet. When
I passed through my night in you, stripped of everything, even my

mother tongue, even the familiar way of thinking that my tongue knows how to mould, the only thing left that was true was the desire for God, made obvious and crystalline by my extreme nudity.

But nudity, like the desire for God, is the exact point where the fact of being numb with cold cohabits with the ecstasy of being alive. Confident nudity is faith.

It's the risk of freezing to death in faith and it's the fact of taking that risk while smiling with happiness.

One day, I decided to leave your country. I phoned the airline, then went back to the empty house and took my suitcase out from under the bed. It was dusty, a scorpion had shed its skin on it. I was in a state of despair close to ecstasy, as if the furthest limit of my sadness were exalting, in a remote corner of my being, the heartbeat of life. The heartbeat of life I remember, stripped of everything with which we dress it, tossed naked onto my pain as if to give it a meaning, as if to direct it towards the time after suffering. I opened the suitcase and left it on the living-room floor for a moment. Stepped into the garden. The sky was grey, heavy, the rain would start any time now, and the harrowing dampness made the flowers look darker than usual, as if they were letting themselves be inhabited from the inside by a secret, impalpable night of splendid density.

In the garden, I spread my arms as wide as I could and looked up at the sky. It was a prayer perhaps, an offering, it was the desperate gift of my own life to life, the hope that the soul of the world would sustain me while, to keep from perishing, my own soul was erased. I was entering deep darkness, but in the midst of my distress, discreetly, a mysterious gratitude flared, an indescribable joy at having been

*brought so far from things that assemble, and so dangerously close
to the bottom of all worlds. Through insults then, I was thanking
heaven. And beneath my revolt against so terrible a wound, I think
that for the first time, I chose to be alive. Not by enduring the kind
of life that is anticipated, not by taking it from waking to waking,
through activities that pass the time, but rather in its perilous
nudity; with utter selflessness, I chose life with its black night and
its white day, chose it fully and letting nothing slip, with my arms
spread wide, in the garden, I accepted everything, all at once — and
all at once, everything accepted me as well — me, a church ruined
by a shiver of patience, a child stuck in an artesian well, a fresco in
fragments on earth that is quaking, a red shovel swallowed by the
sand; I knew, suddenly, that in my pain there also grew the wings of
life, life that moves on without a word, not one, without even saying
my name, yet picking me up by the scruff of the neck, straightening
me up without a sound, and supporting my open arms to keep them
from closing.*

*Because I was leaving your country to keep from collapsing, life,
that evening, greeted me with its blue pungency. I could sense it
clearing a path inside me, distributing its strength to all the hollows
of need so that the terrible plane by which your face would be erased
would take off.*

Marco is still asleep. In sheer compensation, Marianne is
eating some bread while she packs. She is eating bread, then
all at once she doesn't want anything and she starts to cry.
Fulli gets up and approaches her on the tips of his paws.

She holds out her hand, he licks it, then licks it more and more frantically and so energetically that Marianne ends up laughing. Then Fulli sits down and cocks his head. "Mission accomplished," he thinks. He sits there, motionless, watching Marianne. He really does know how to smile, she'd never noticed till now. She offers him the bread, which he hasn't asked for. In the memory of her that he'll hang onto, she will be simply herself, with nothing to criticize. Fulli will be the only one to remember Marianne. He won't phone. He won't write. Yet he'll be the one and only lost friend.

That night, with exceptional kindness, Marco's mother prepares a stuffed turtledove. No one's really hungry but she does it with the utmost diligence, to leave a happy memory in Marianne's stomach, to celebrate or to console herself on her departure. Marianne struggles to swallow her portion. The mother offers her another, which Marianne turns down. Then, in an outrageous act of regression, the mother dumps the whole contents of the pan on her plate. It's her final exercise of power and her final act of generosity. Marianne submits. Eats.

On television, there are slow-motion images of the earthquake. The vault collapses and rises up to heaven like a cloud. The light soul of St. Francis, finally released from the architecture made to contain his enlightenment, disappears through the gaping hole of the church, above the altar, and the camera trembles in the sigh of his liberation.

The wind reveals neither where it has come from nor

where it is going. It meets no resistance, depending on what direction an invisible power pushes it; the wind itself is that power, it turns without breaking, crosses the street wherever it wants, asks no one for anything. A total presence in this continual departure, it is everywhere at once, yet it is here and now and tomorrow again, effortlessly.

Marco has been patrolling his village for years. Women travellers find their way into his bed, but none will agree to marry his village, his mother, his dozens of uncles and cousins — precisely because they are travellers. Marco is true to himself, he lets them go, he remembers their passage as a benign burn, knowing already that his peculiar way of being both root and leaf will prevent him always from going with them. Marco's soul is like that of Francis held in his basilica, prisoner of a solidly medieval architecture, and the earth only trembles after seven hundred years.

Marianne, in front of the TV set between Marco, his mother, and the stuffed turtledove, is watching for the fifteenth time the collapse of the basilica's vault. A tear falls onto her plate, adding a little salt. A tear for the happiness of Francis, a tear for the vanity of human architectures, a tear for Marco embedded in his village, and a tear for herself, who will fly away tomorrow, with her faith totally demolished, with her desire suspended, with the small amount of strength she has left to thwart the temptations of a last-minute hope, and try to hope that hope will be possible somewhere else.

Everything is difficult now. Francis's soul rises up to the

sky along with the dust of the vault, you can see the heavy stone shatter on the ground, its fragments added to those of the fresco in an appalling disorder. The ground is scattered with debris. Few of us are able to fly.

When I close my eyes, I no longer see your face. I see the lake. I see Fulli, who comes running when I knock on the door, I see a scar on your left forearm, I see your back relax all at once when sleep overcomes you. I see a glass of lemonade and my thirst seeking it, I see hammered copper trays, the night; I see distinctly the candlesticks on the tables, the wild boar in its sauce, the circles of oil around tomatoes, the circles of oil around boats, I see men at the top of a ladder, shaking an olive tree. I hear olives falling into their out-stretched nets, my own teeth biting into a perfect apple, and I hear the desert widening between us, all the way to the last words murmured in the dark so tears will stay hidden.

I hear the last night passing over our motionless skins and your insomniac body watching over us in silence. Hold me in your arms all night, the bedroom was blue and the window open, through the sheer curtain the stars took on impossible dimensions, and you even got up to check that we were still on earth. I hear your voice saying half the words and in spite of everything, the words alight on my heart. I hear very clearly the last night drawing to a close, with no respect for my distress, I hear the rooster's cry make a sound like crystal, I hear the wool of the blankets slipping, reptilian, I hear your eyes open when I open mine, your eyes wide open, your eyes never closed, your eyes that since the night before haven't stopped looking at the huge star sewn into the fabric of the curtain. I hear myself tell you that I want to be in your arms, and I hear you tell me that I've spent the night there, and I hear you growing old while I zip my suitcase, I barely touch my pain with my fingertips, I entrust myself to time. That morning, like all other mornings, smelled of rosemary, dew and dust.

You told me: "I knew I'd lose you, the way I lost the dogs before you. You're right. I have to learn to let all of you go. One day maybe you'll come back this way, we'll be old and it won't matter, what matters is that we have recognized each other."

THE GREAT HAPPINESS

*S*hortly before I left, a woman had knocked on the garden gate. She was dressed in turquoise silk with no underwear: a febrile, slightly scattered woman whom I'd met by chance and invited, without really thinking she'd come, to drop in for tea in the empty house I had no tea to offer her, I gave her a glass of water, and we sat in a square of sunlight. With no introduction whatsoever she told me about a friend of hers who'd spent years doing nothing but walk. What does he do? He walks. What do you do? Me? I walk. He doesn't have a house. He eats whatever he finds — hazelnuts, apples, peaches, mushrooms. When she's in the area, she locates him by tracking the plants of mint whose leaves he's eaten. He eats what he finds when he finds it, whether he's hungry or not. In summer, he sleeps under trees or in caves, in winter he squats in a house of which some unknown person always leaves one wing open. Before, he also *played music, he still carves flutes sometimes. Apparently he never lacks for anything.*

What a pointless life, how dirty he must be. Psychiatrists would surely have a suitable diagnosis.

And then you wonder if the man really does live a marginal life or if, on the contrary, he's at the centre of things. At the centre of the necessary mint. Without the fear of loss that is associated with owning. Then you wonder where you are yourself. You realize that you'd forgotten the fabulous coincidence of the mushroom given, the natural connection between the need to eat and the fact of finding some edible growths on the ground. Generosity, in the end, cannot be a coincidence. The mushroom grows because he'll come along to pick it. It's for him that the cave is empty, that the wing of a house is open, for him as well that the apple made the nonchalant effort to become an apple. Everything is in order. He asks no one for anything, neither money nor lodging nor work: nothing. He takes the things that are offered him, they are no more his than another's, they are there, that's all: there's an apple, I'm hungry, I take it, it's neither fair nor unfair that it comes to me, it comes to me, basta. The anonymity of living things is a fundamental fact. He doesn't take, he recognizes. Recognizes the apple in its vocation of apple and himself in his own hunger. He is in the order of things.

He represents a rare, essential, anonymous witness. Of what? Of nothing. Precisely. His life is devoid of all the things that fill our lives, yet it goes on. It is something that, compared with useful activities, always risks being forgotten. It is the possibility, stubbornly postponed, of being merely one's existing self. As if living were enough to make one alive. As if humans were asked to do nothing but honour the unassuming offerings of nature.

Nothing else is asked for.

Extreme asceticism speaks a terrifying truth for those of us who work so that we won't die tomorrow; it's that we won't die tomorrow in any case. It's that in any case, even if we were to die tomorrow, it would be another trivial event in the order of things. We should keep going with an animal trust in life's resolute affection for itself. There will be food and there will be drink.

It's a truth that is as ample and light as the turquoise woman sitting with her glass of water, yet a heavy truth too, because it collides with acquired knowledge, with the surreal, contradictory, terrifying collage of prescriptions for being. Our convictions weave a net and when we try to free ourselves from it, in many cases the effort itself becomes part of the weave. Which is normal. There's no precise rule about existence. That walking man undermines the work we do every minute, he makes us suspect that maybe there's no charge for the fact of being alive. Terrifying: there may be no other meaning for existence but the simple fact of existing. A grandiose fact. A miracle repeated unobtrusively by every springtime on earth, by every morning. To owe nothing to life and, for that very reason, owe it everything, that is to say: owe it life itself.

After she's told the story of the man who walks, the turquoise woman puts down her glass, stands up, and says goodbye; she's going to catch a train that will take her home, to Rome, where she teaches Latin to teens.

We humans have struggled against the progress of time. We have looked at nature and even though he has seen evidence, we have succumbed to the temptation of the malignant Eternity that is defined negatively, that is the opposite of becoming; we have succumbed to the temptation of the Certainty which helps us neither to love nor to die, rather helps us forget the sadness implicit in both love and death. And there we are, incapable of a faith that has no need of Certainty and Eternity. Yet true faith is blind, which is its virtue and its great beauty. In that sense, it is a form of love, love being nothing but a sudden gathering of strength in preparation for absolute risk. Love is blind, by definition. Love, by definition, is a journey courageously aimed in the direction of uncertainty. When this Certainty appears to protect us from the fall, love is on the decline.

True eternity is not a duel with becoming. It is conditional to the passage of time, and, to gain access to it, one need only place an empty chair in the path of things, so that it can sit down and, while seated, open the peace and quiet that belongs to it. It would be enough to expect nothing from it, it would even be enough not to wait for it, since waiting would mean making it disappear again behind the time that is so obviously passing. Eternity would be that of being present to oneself. Not to oneself as a closed and suspicious entity, but like winter, like the lake, like the feather. Eternity would be nothing but the fruit of a true presence.

You restored to me a childhood still intact in spite of what school and work had made of it. You restored a childhood of games and astonishment, the childhood that accepts from the outset everything it sees, because what it sees astonishes it, and astonishment gives it pleasure without excess. Our bed was that empty chair where eternity came to settle, and precisely because I knew that I'd have to leave soon, tomorrow, because our time would be brief, eternity came and sat on the chair, came to tell me when I was crumbling and bereft of my own language: take a good look at him, he has always been there, you loved him in advance, and after you leave, he'll be there always, you won't stop loving him.

There was the art of presence, you were its prince and you taught it to me in secret when I thought I was waiting for you. That waiting for you which caused me so much suffering held a promise that unlike ordinary promises didn't need a future. There was faith. My awareness of it was sudden and abrupt, though the faith was very ancient; a prehistoric faith, a faith forever young in our surprising story, once upon a time there was a faith that took on your voice to knock on my door and when, blind, I opened it, I understood at the same time that I'd lost you and that nothing is ever lost, that everything accompanies us in the madness of love. Since that time, since all times at once, I have been my own life, which is to say, the universe. I follow in the footsteps of an absence that love forces me to examine head-on, and where I find, when I am strong enough, the great beauty of poems that no one can write.

I've changed the time on all the clocks, it's spring now in my country. I prefer that feast to the feast of your language, which surprises me, pleases me. Your name has gone back to being the name of a man. Truth escapes from it. I have walked on words written as if they were stones, I didn't know how broad was the water to be crossed, the shore is close now, I'm surprised. I arrive home, I forget nothing about you, without you I remember everything, and holding that memory in my hands I see that they've stopped shaking. My faith has followed me. Perhaps it arrived at night, entered surreptitiously, it is there in front of me as I write these lines, it points to the edges of the sidewalk where the snow opened onto the long-awaited soil.

I have not stopped loving you. I don't intend to stop loving you. You're busy elsewhere. It's April, you walk your dogs earlier and earlier. You rarely think about me. It's chilly. All is well. You don't even have a cold. Soon you'll shave your beard. My country is vast, I dream every night. I have lost you. I'm relieved. I won't have to lose you again. I won't have to step again into the dizziness of that loss, in whose depths stuffed ducks and dogs that look like snowballs are playing. I am here.

My body taken away from your body, my soul a soul minus yours: I was a subtraction. Today I exist like a prime number, indivisible, alone, on one paw, one, round, three, seven. Eleven, thirteen: you no longer have a hold on the taste of soup.

I sit in the middle of happiness as if on a hardwood floor that creaks and swells in the sun. I am sitting where the light is at its white centre. In that great happiness there is a great misfortune too. It is like the kernel of happiness. It is the misfortune of life that moves and that by moving causes pain. Happiness asks to move along with life, it requires that perfect circles be broken.

She sits in the middle of happiness, surprised that she's been able to travel so far.